· NEXUS ·

ALISON MORTON

Pulcheria
Press

Published in 2019 by Pulcheria Press
Copyright © 2019 by Alison Morton
All rights reserved Tous droits réservés

The right of Alison Morton to be identified as the author of this work has been asserted in accordance with the Copyright, Designs and Patents Acts 1988 Sections 77 and 78.

No part of this book may be reproduced, stored in a retrieval system or transmitted in any form or by any means, electronic, mechanical, photocopying, recording or otherwise, without prior written permission of the copyright holder, except for the use of brief quotations in a book review.

Propriété littéraire d'Alison Morton
Tous droits de reproduction, d'adaptation et de traduction, intégrale ou partielle réservés pour tous pays. L'auteur ou l'éditeur est seul propriétaire des droits et responsable du contenu de ce livre.

Le Code de la propriété intellectuelle interdit les copies ou reproductions destinées à une utilisation collective. Toute représentation ou reproduction intégrale ou partielle faite par quelque procédé que ce soit, sans le consentement de l'auteur ou de ses ayant droit ou ayant cause, est illicite et constitue une contrefaçon, aux termes des articles L.335-2 et suivants du Code de la propriété intellectuelle

This is a work of fiction. Names, characters, places, incidents are either products of the author's imagination or used fictitiously. Any resemblance to actual events, locations or persons living or dead is entirely coincidental.

ISBN 9791097310202

PRAISE FOR THE ROMA NOVA SERIES

INCEPTIO
"Brilliantly plotted original story, grippingly told and cleverly combining the historical with the futuristic. It's a real edge-of-the-seat read, genuinely hard to put down." – Sue Cook

CARINA
"This is a fabulous thriller that cracks along at a great pace and just doesn't let up from start to finish." – Discovering Diamonds Reviews

PERFIDITAS
"Alison Morton has built a fascinating, exotic world! Carina's a bright, sassy detective with a winning dry sense of humour. The plot is pretty snappy too!" – Simon Scarrow

SUCCESSIO
"I thoroughly enjoyed this classy thriller, the third in Morton's epic series set in Roma Nova." – Caroline Sanderson in *The Bookseller*

AURELIA
"AURELIA explores a 1960s that is at once familiar and utterly different – a brilliant page turner that will keep you gripped from first page to last. Highly recommended." – Russell Whitfield

INSURRECTIO
"INSURRECTIO – a taut, fast-paced thriller. I enjoyed it enormously. Rome, guns and rebellion. Darkly gripping stuff." – Conn Iggulden

RETALIO
"RETALIO is a terrific concept engendering passion, love and loyalty. I actually cheered aloud." – J J Marsh

ROMA NOVA EXTRA
"One of the reasons I am enthralled with the Roma Nova series is the concept of the whole thing." – Helen Hollick, Vine Voice

THE ROMA NOVA THRILLERS
The Carina Mitela adventures
INCEPTIO
CARINA (novella)
PERFIDITAS
SUCCESSIO

The Aurelia Mitela adventures
AURELIA
NEXUS (novella)
INSURRECTIO
RETALIO

ROMA NOVA EXTRA (Short stories)

ABOUT THE AUTHOR

A 'Roman nut' since age eleven, Alison Morton has clambered over much of Roman Europe.

Armed with an MA in history, six years' military service and a love of thrillers, she explores via her Roma Nova novels the 'what if' idea of a modern Roman society run by strong women.

Alison lives in France with her husband, cultivates a Roman herb garden and drinks wine.

Find out more at alison-morton.com, follow her on Twitter @alison_morton and Facebook (AlisonMortonAuthor)

DRAMATIS PERSONAE

Mitela family
Aurelia Mitela – Diplomat, sometime government investigator, ex-Praetorian Guard Special Forces (PGSF)
Marina Mitela – Aurelia's young daughter
Miklós Farkas – Aurelia's life companion

Roma Nova Government
Tertullius Plico – Imperial Secretary, external security affairs
Paulinus Axius – Junior officer, Foreign Ministry

London legation
Burnus – Captain, PGSF, diplomatic detail
Furnia – *Optio*, PGSF, diplomatic detail
Rubrius, Legal *consultor* (lawyer)

United Kingdom
Harry Carter – Senior official, Foreign Office
Tom Carter – His son
Maury Finer – Employee at Thurswick Stud
Davy Finer – Maury's brother
Linda Casely – An unpleasant schoolgirl
John Casely – Linda's older brother
'Raincoat Man'

Rome legation
Bellania – Senior centurion, PGSF, diplomatic detail
Galus – Legal *consultor*

Rome – other
Agent Bianchi – Italian security services
Major Pirozzi – *Carabinieri*, Rome

Vienna legation
Licinia – Captain, PGSF, diplomatic detail

Vienna - other
David Soane – Aurelia's cousin and local manager of Soane's
Oberleutnant Hartl – Vienna *Gendarmerie*
Barbara Teiderstein – Hotel owner

Paris legation
Celcus – Captain, PGSF, diplomatic detail

Paris - other
Régis Morin – Investigator, French internal security services
Duvalier – Field agent, French internal security services

1

'I've lost him, Aurelia.'

Harry Carter's voice was low, toneless, but I could hear the despair in his restrained British voice. Given the time of day, he must have been calling from his panelled office at the British Foreign Ministry.

'Are you absolutely sure?' I said. 'He could just be on one of his walkabouts.'

'His tutor at Cambridge said he hasn't been in college for six weeks.'

Hades. What could I say? I stared at my yellow office wall and tried to compose a tactful answer.

At seventeen, Tom Carter had been a classical surly teenager. Harry had invited me to dinner one evening five years ago when I'd been posted to our London legation as political officer. It was a third level posting in the Roma Novan diplomatic hierarchy, but a restful one for me after a very fraught intelligence operation in Berlin. I'd taken to Harry immediately, not only for his connections as a senior spook – that was part of my job – but for his friendliness to a newcomer on the circuit and for his sense of uprightness.

Over an after-dinner brandy Harry had confided that his son Tom had been away for three days with no contact. During the evening, he'd kept looking at the hallway.

'Do you want me to go, Harry?' I'd said eventually.

'No, please don't. I'm probably fussing.' He'd changed the subject, but fidgeted, glancing at his watch when he thought I wouldn't notice.

'He always comes back, usually broke. Young men, eh?' He attempted to laugh.

Just as I stood to go ten minutes later, the sound of the front door opening echoed from the hall and Tom had shuffled in; dirty, dishevelled, eye sockets brown with exhaustion. He shrugged as his father hugged him, grunted and went upstairs without a word.

That was five years ago. I'd been home and then taken a posting in the Eastern United States since then. Now I was filling in here in London for our UK *nuncia*, our ambassador, who'd been taken ill.

'Have you informed the civil police?' I winced as I asked such an obvious question.

'You know I can't do that.'

'Harry, it's no shame. For a government functionary like you, they would be discreet.'

'Don't bet on it. One of those bloody tabloids would get hold of it if they paid enough.'

'That's a bit cynical.' But he was right. Their press here in the UK was outrageous. But then so was the *Sol Populi* at home.

'Can't you use your people in your security service to get somebody to take a look?'

Silence.

'Harry?'

'Completely off the record, Aurelia, I had two retired officers nose around, but they found nothing.' He coughed. 'Not a trace, which was odd. I can't use anybody active. Imagine the stink if the parliamentary oversight committee got wind of it.'

I smiled at his schoolboy half-pun. But I knew he was desperately trying to cover his distress. Under that gruff exterior his heart was breaking.

'Tom is an adult, Harry. You're not responsible for him or his actions.' That sounded so hollow. Harry loved his only child unconditionally. Since his wife Valerie had died, he'd lavished all his love on Tom. Almost too much. He'd kept Tom close as a child and not allowed him to fly on his own. He'd traipsed with him through northern hills on walking trips, taken him all over Europe in the school holidays, once even to Roma Nova. But the holidays were snatched in small gaps in Harry's intense working life as he rose steadily in his government's service.

Nothing had seemed to please Tom the times I'd seen him. Bent shoulders and floppy blond hair either side of a widow's peak had framed a persistently unsmiling mouth. But once, and only that one time after we'd returned to Roma Nova after my first London posting when he came out to our farm at Castra Lucilla, did I see his nondescript face break out a smile. His eyes sparkled and he stood straight as he gripped the paddock fence following every move inside it.

Miklós, my companion, was lunging one of his 'ventures', a young, dark bay filly that oozed quality and was very obviously of Hungarian/thoroughbred cross-breeding: fine lines but with a hint of a stockier build and strength. English thoroughbreds were bred as lightweight speed machines; these potential 'sport horses', as Miklós called them, were more robust, with stamina for endurance, but grace for performance.

When I'd first given him management of the stud in Essex, Miklós had said he wanted to breed his Hungarian stallion, Bátor, now retired to a life of fat-bellied ease at Castra Lucilla, with some of the thoroughbred mares in the hope of producing some quality animals as prospective sport horses – eventers, dressage, show jumping; that sort of thing.

I remember raising a sceptical eyebrow and asking, 'Would such a venture be profitable?'

In my mind I saw again that cocksure glimmer sparkling in his eyes. 'Quality unbroken youngstock can fetch a sizeable four-figure sum.'

At the end of the long lunge line, the young horse had been trotting in a wide circle around Miklós. He'd seen me leaning on the exercise arena's rails with Harry and Tom and in his own crooning tongue had brought the horse to a walk and then a halt. Gathering up the long line, he'd brought her in to him, praising her all the while, rewarded her with a carrot which he'd fished from his jacket pocket and then led her over to me.

I'd looked up into his dark eyes. The sun filtering through his black curls and the knowing grin on his tanned face made me swallow hard.

'Oh, hi,' I recovered. 'How's it going?'

'She's enjoying her schooling,' he said. 'Soon we will introduce her to carrying a saddle, then start gently backing her – leaning over her first, then quietly sitting on her, getting her used to carrying weight and someone upright astride her. After that we'll turn her away to grass for a few months to think about what she has learnt.'

And he had winked at me – a hidden meaning? What *I* had learnt maybe? I felt the warmth creep up my neck. Gods, he was going to pay for that.

'You remember Harry Carter from London from when I was posted there?' I said in English, waving my fingers towards the father and son.

'Of course.' He nodded at Harry, then turned to Tom. 'And who is this?'

For the next three days, Tom hardly left the saddle. When he did, he willingly set to cleaning tack, grooming and mucking out stables alongside Miklós. We had plenty of farmworkers, including stable hands, but Miklós insisted on looking after his own horses when we were at the farm. He said it was the best way to get to know them, to form a bond of partnership. 'Get to know every hair and whisker on a horse, then things that go wrong will not be missed – cuts, lameness, colic – give a horse your all and he'll give you twice, three times, as much back.'

'I've never seen Tom so happy, Aurelia,' Harry said as he and I sat on the veranda at the back of the farmhouse one evening and watched the man instructing the boy in the paddock. Miklós looked up and waved at me across the lawn. I raised my glass half full of our estate wine to him and smiled.

'Leave Tom with us for a few weeks, or months if you want,' I said. 'I'm here in Roma Nova for a few months now, possibly a year, before my next posting abroad. We'll be in the city some of the time and Miklós would keep an eye on him there as well. See it as a gap year.'

I smiled but he didn't reciprocate.

'Your husband is a caring man and I think he genuinely likes Tom, but I couldn't possibly intrude on your life like that.'

I smiled at Harry's calling Miklós my husband. He knew perfectly well we hadn't married. Few Roma Novan women did. We didn't need to as our names and property descended to our daughters whatever our social arrangements. But Harry was a very traditional British man.

'I mean it, Harry,' I said. 'Miklós loves nothing better than somebody who shares his love of horses.'

'Thank you, but no. Tom has his place at Cambridge in a few weeks' time. I'll buy him a horse in the meantime and perhaps you can rent me a place for it at your stud farm near there.'

That was then. Miklós had heard a year ago from the Thurswick Stud manager, Lambert, that Tom had turned up there occasionally, but most of the time the staff had exercised his horse. As soon as we'd arrived in the UK a few weeks ago for me to fill in for the *nuncia*, Miklós had driven up there. He discovered that Tom had instructed them to sell the horse; he'd pocketed the proceeds. I didn't have the heart to mention it to Harry, but he must have known when the stabling bills stopped arriving in the post.

Miklós had thought Tom needed to be left on his own, to be away from Harry, but said he didn't want to interfere between father and son. His own upbringing on the Hungarian Plains had been harsh with a father freer with a belt than with love.

Now back in the present, I tried to think what I could do for Harry.

'Look, I'll check with Miklós to see if Tom's been in contact since we arrived. Miklós has been at the stud for a few days and he'll be back there again next week. I haven't heard anything, but I don't poke around in Miklós's affairs.'

'That's very kind, Aurelia. Really appreciated.'

'Do I have to come as well?' Miklós was sitting on the bed watching me while he towelled his hair. He'd arrived from Essex only twenty-five minutes ago after driving through terrible evening traffic. He'd stripped off his check shirt, moleskins and boots and dived straight in the shower.

'No, of course not.' I smiled at him. I was due at a cocktail party at the French Embassy in half an hour. Miklós would never be a diplomatic spouse, smiling at inanities and hiding his true feelings, and I would never demand that of him. He lived in the horse world where he'd become respected for his expertise from the king's own trainer at the royal stud right down to the itinerant horse dealers who travelled round Britain and Ireland.

'Just zip me up, though,' I said. As his fingers tucked the tiny tab into the top of the seam to conceal it, his other hand rested on my shoulder. He bent down and kissed the nape of my neck. A warm tingle flowed down my spine. I wouldn't be back late. I turned, laid my hand on his bare forearm and kissed him quickly on the lips. It would have to do. I bent and picked up my sequinned evening bag and slipped my compact and lipstick inside. The briefing note would wait until I was sitting in the back of the car.

'Miklós, one thing before I go…'

'Yes?'

'Have you picked up any news of Tom Carter?'

At the reception, I managed to keep up a genuine-looking smile *'Mais non, Monsieur l'Ambassadeur,* I would be delighted!'

Oh, gods, I'd somehow promised to host a families' games day in our legation gardens. They were large enough, situated on the site of the old Roman *castra* behind the seventeenth-century mansion nestling against the remains of the original London Wall. When the legation was being rebuilt after London's Great Fire, the Roma Novan *nuncia* of the time had bought the plot next door. Astute woman! It had been covered in charred timbers and smoking stones for weeks according to the legation histories. Her actions had not only safeguarded two of the original third century towers then, but also prevented them being demolished, along with a lot of the wall, in the following century. Now in the mid 1970s, the London Corporation was falling over itself to preserve even the tiniest portion of wall as 'heritage'. The irony of it.

'Please call me Gustave, *madame.*'

'Only if you call me Aurelia.'

His smile was so French; generous yet restrained. A charmer and knowing it, Gustave d'Egigny was nevertheless sharp-witted and, according to my head of station, extremely well connected in Napoleon's imperial court as well as inside the French administration. Harry Carter said it was safest to treat him like a cross between delicate Sèvres china and an anaconda. He thought d'Egigny must have studied poker-playing to professional level when he was pursuing his master's degree at the elite Paris business school. Perhaps so, but at the moment Gustave d'Egigny was putting out friendly diplomatic feelers.

'Very well, Aurelia. That is agreed. My assistant will contact yours to arrange matters. Will you be able to show us some of your Roman life?'

'Perhaps, Gustave, but we are very much a modern country.'

'But, of course.' He gave me a slight bow and left. I kept the smile on my face, but sighed inside. Everybody was still fascinated by the ancient Romans even fifteen hundred years on and thought we still went around in full segmented armour or togas. Well, I wasn't going to force our people to dress up for a diplomatic community party, unless they particularly wanted to wear traditional dress.

'How's it going?' A friendly, solid voice in this brittle web of insincerity.

'Harry, I'm so pleased to see you.'

'I saw d'Egigny was doing his charm act on you. Anything interesting?'

I laughed. 'No, I've just agreed to host an event. But you're right – he was making a particular effort to be nice. Don't get me wrong, we have good relations with the French, these days but I don't think they've really forgiven us yet for pressuring this emperor's grandfather back across the Rhine.'

'Ha! How the hell did you do that? I suppose it was Justina's mother?'

'You can't expect me to gossip about the imperatrix of Roma Nova, Harry, but let's say her Aunt Antonia was an extremely effective *nuncia* in Paris with a persuasive manner.'

'Which tells me nothing at all!'

'Knowing people's secrets is our currency in kind. It's helped us survive all these years.'

'Well, we all know your spies are the best.'

'Spies?' I raised my eyebrow in mock surprise.

'Don't kid me, woman.' He grinned at me, then chuckled. I was so pleased to see him laugh. He calmed, then keeping his gaze straight ahead and nodding at the other guests as they circulated, he said, 'I don't suppose you have anything for me personally?'

I touched his forearm with my free hand.

'Nothing, I'm afraid. Miklós is making a few enquiries.'

The expression on Harry's face hardly changed, but a blink of pain in his eyes told me enough. I vowed that once this temporary assignment was finished, I'd take a few days' leave and go and find this irritating young man. And I'd drag him back by his hair if necessary.

2

To my disappointment, Miklós wasn't at the legation when I returned. A scrawled note written on lined paper torn from a spiral-bound pad lay on my pillow. *Gone to see some cousins. They may have heard whispers about Tom. Back in a few days.* I folded it up and shoved it into my bedside cabinet drawer before flopping down onto my side of the bed. 'Cousins' for him included almost any wanderer who owned a horse across the whole of Europe. The gods knew when he'd return. I took a good, deep breath, then pulled myself to my feet.

It was only half past nine, but Marina would be fast asleep. Or should be. At eleven, my daughter was starting to assert herself a little. I crept along the corridor to her small suite, opened the door as quietly as I could. Marina's nurse, Aemilia, was reading a magazine, her head nodding rhythmically. Black wires ran from headphones with sponge pads to her new portable cassette player. The music was evidently too loud for her to have heard me. I walked towards her as obviously as I could and waved my hand.

She jerked her head up and her mouth fell open. Her face was a picture of dismay as she ripped off the headphones and stood up.

'I'm sorry, *domina*,' she stuttered. 'I didn't hear you come in.'

'Don't worry, Aemilia. Please. Sit down and carry on reading. I'm just going to pop in and see Marina. I expect she's asleep, so I won't disturb her.'

'She was when I looked in an hour ago, but she's a little restless. I think she's still finding the new school difficult. But they're doing some extra English with her and she's making good progress, so they say.'

'Well, let her run around the gardens tomorrow and get some fresh air. She can skip her dancing lesson if you think she's too tired.'

Aemilia looked away and said nothing.

'Is there anything else?' I asked.

'Not really, *domina*.'

'Aemilia, you've been with us several years now. Please say what you mean.'

'I think she would enjoy some more time with you. Just the two of you.'

'Thank you, Aemilia. That's very honest. I'll say goodnight now and won't disturb you when I leave.' Despite my words I knew I was being abrupt when I saw the younger woman flush. Her words hurt. I'd asked for it and had got it straight between the eyes. But all Roma Novan women worked. Even here in the United Kingdom it was becoming more acceptable, although most mothers stayed at home if they could. Perhaps Aemilia was becoming affected by the other mostly British women she was chatting to while waiting at the pupils' entrance at the school door. I'd try and take and collect Marina myself this next week.

I crept in and closed the door softly behind me. Even in the dim nightlight, the garish wallpaper and bright, large, patterned green curtains were hardly restful, nor was the bright rainbow bedspread, but Marina liked them. She turned over and opened one eye.

'Mama?'

'Shush, darling, you should be asleep.'

She pulled herself out of the nest of pink sheets and white blankets and crooked her elbow to support her head. She pushed her fine hair back, but several strands escaped. I knelt down by the bed.

'I'm not sleepy.' She looked down.

'Is there something special bothering you?'

'How long are we going to stay here?'

'Here in London? Just a few weeks.'

'Oh. Good. Do I have to go to school, then? Can't I just be on holiday? Or do lessons with Aemilia?'

'What's happened, sweetheart?'

She burst into tears. I gathered her into my arms. After a few moments, she calmed.

'Tell me.'

At eight the next morning, grasping Marina's hand, I walked out of the back door of the legation building. My Praetorian escort, *Optio* Furnia, unlocked the heavy wooden gate in the wall. The three of us walked across the grass to the pedestrian bridge, up the steps, then alongside the small green which led to the school front courtyard. I pushed open the glass doors into the lobby covered in sleek beechwood panelling. Anybody else might have been impressed by shields and silver cups in cupboards lining the walls and the soft lighting illuminating the school coat of arms, but I wasn't here to admire achievements.

'Can I help you, madam?' the receptionist asked. She glanced nervously at Furnia's sturdy figure behind me in her severely cut purple Praetorian suit.

'Countess Mitela to see the headmistress, if you please.'

'I'll just ring through. Please take a seat.'

I remained standing, watching her as she spoke rapidly into her handset. Her free hand played with the curled cable.

A door catch clicked along the corridor and a slim woman with a long face and white pageboy haircut walked towards me, her hand outstretched.

'Delighted to see you again, countess. Please come into my office.' She glanced down at my daughter. 'Perhaps Marina would like to join her class while we talk.'

The little hand clasped mine tighter.

'No, this concerns her and I wish her to stay.'

'Very well.' Her face tightened as she glanced at Furnia, but she gestured to the two chairs on the other side of her desk. I turned to my escort. 'You can wait outside in the corridor, Furnia. I'm sure we'll be perfectly safe in Miss Buckley's office.'

She took one last look around, nodded and left. The headmistress didn't quite sigh, but her face relaxed a little.

'Now, Miss Buckley, I think you have a problem that needs nipping in the bud,' I began. 'While I accept you are doing all you can to support Marina, not every one of her fellow pupils is as generous. You have one called Casely, Linda. I suggest you call her in for a little talk.'

'Has there been a problem between the two girls?' She seemed genuinely surprised. 'Linda offered to look after Marina.'

'I would not be here otherwise,' I replied. I turned to my daughter. 'Please tell Miss Buckley what you told me.'

Marina gave me a scared look. I nodded and gave her hand a squeeze. She then pushed her shoulders back, sat up and looked straight at Miss Buckley.

'Linda Casely laughs at me in front of her friends. She pinches me when I do not obey her. She stole my new pen.' Marina gulped, but folded her hands in her lap.

'These are serious things to say, Marina,' Miss Buckley stared at her. 'Are you sure you haven't misunderstood?'

'No. Roma Novans do not lie.' She returned the headmistress's stare without flinching. I was so proud of her. But when she pulled up the sleeve of her uniform shirt and showed the two bruise marks, anger assaulted me again.

'Well, Miss Buckley,' I said, keeping my voice as steady as I could. 'I think you need to have Casely in and to search her satchel.'

We waited in the lobby around the corner from Miss Buckley's office. Marina and I sat on the yellow-ochre visitor easy chairs while Furnia stood silently watching everything. Footsteps, one light, one heavier. A click of the headmistress's door and I heard a child crying. A pause of five minutes. Another click of the door and a child sobbing. I stood and held my hand out to Marina. The rules could go and hang; I wanted to see this little piece of maliciousness. Seizing Marina's hand, I left the lobby with her and turned into the corridor.

'Stop,' I said to the woman and child retreating down the corridor. They both turned. 'Linda Casely?'

The girl nodded. Her eyes narrowed and she flinched. She was Marina's height, but tubby, her skirt belt overflowed by a bulging shirt. Her shoulder-length hair held by an Alice band framed a round face with small brown eyes.

'This is most irregular,' the teacher accompanying her said. 'I must protest at —'

'Do as you wish, teacher,' I interrupted. 'But your pupil must apologise to my daughter.'

'That's for the headmistress to decide.'

'No, best done now and quickly,' I replied. We weren't in Roma Nova, but restorative justice was still a good principle. A little embarrassment and a warning often brought effective results. A bell sounded and girls emerged from doors along the corridor. Some of them slowed and gave us curious looks.

'Countess.' Miss Buckley's voice. She stood in her doorway. 'Would you all come into my office, please? You too, Miss Johns, and the two girls.'

Miss Johns and I sat in front of the headmistress's desk. Marina stood close by my side and eyed the other girl who now seemed more composed.

'All I require, Miss Buckley, is that Linda Casely apologises to my daughter and promises to behave civilly towards her.'

'She has told me she is sorry and won't do it again.' Miss Johns looked at me as if I were extracting tribute in body weight. 'That should be enough.'

'Well, I think that as she has admitted her fault to you, she should find no difficulty in apologising directly to Marina.'

'Do I have to?' Linda whined.

'Linda,' Miss Buckley said. 'Please wait to speak until I ask you.' The girl shot her a resentful look but then stared at the floor as Miss Buckley fixed her with a steady eye. The headmistress turned to me. 'Is a formal apology necessary?' She was trying to convey something with her look but I couldn't work out exactly what. If I hadn't seen what a confident presence she had, I would have thought it was nervousness. The quick glance she exchanged with Johns confirmed it.

'Yes, I think so. It will take a few seconds.' I turned to Linda. 'Come now, make your apology, then we can all get on with our day.'

The girl glanced at Miss Buckley who nodded.

'Sorry,' she mumbled.

'I think you can do a little better than that, Linda.' I frowned at her. 'You need to say it to Marina, to say what you're apologising for and promise not to do it again. Try again.'

The girl stuck her chin out and pinched her lips together.

'Well, Linda?' Miss Buckley said.

'Caselys don't apologise to nobody!' she blurted out. The two teachers stared with appalled expressions at the defiant child. Neither moved or even blinked for a second. They evidently weren't used to such behaviour at their genteel school for young ladies.

I recovered first.

'Linda, even the strongest of us have to apologise sometimes in our lives,' I said. 'Come, child, make your apology and take the lesson now while you're young.' I looked at her, not in anger now, but in sorrow that her mother hadn't taught her better. The girl puckered her mouth as if she were eating bitter herbs, then turned towards Marina and half closed her eyes. There was no mistake about the animosity in them. Marina shrank back.

'Sorry if you felt upset about anything I've done or said,' Linda recited mechanically. 'I didn't mean none of it.'

Nor did she mean any of her words now. But I had to acknowledge that we weren't going to get any further.

'Very well,' I said. 'Marina, do you accept Linda's apology?'

Marina shot a glance at me then faced her nemesis.

'I accept,' she said in a strained voice.

'Good. Now you and Linda should shake hands… in the English way,' I reminded Marina in case she thought she had to use the forearm handshake. I couldn't put her through that close a contact.

Linda left with Miss Johns, but just as she went through the doorway, she turned and shot me a defiant look. 'I'm telling my brother of you.'

'That's enough, Linda,' Miss Buckley snapped. 'Back to your class.'

After a moment staring at the door as if to make sure some presence was no longer lingering there, Miss Buckley turned back to me.

'I do apologise for that child's poor behaviour. It's a sad case – her mother died a year ago in tragic circumstances. I can't say any more.' The headmistress glanced at me, then Marina. 'Now, Marina. Why don't we find you a different friend? What about Susanne, the Swedish girl?'

After watching Marina almost skipping down the corridor hand in hand with the tall blonde girl who smiled down at her, I turned to Miss Buckley.

'Who *is* Linda's brother? Another child?'

'Unfortunately, not. John Casely is the son of Linda's father's first wife. He was released from prison a month ago after serving four years for armed robbery.' She paused. 'He was only eighteen when he went in. He came here two weeks ago to make sure Linda was being "treated right," he said.' She looked away and bit her bottom lip. 'Their father, urged on by Linda's mother, I suspect, gave a generous donation towards the school several years ago. He wanted his daughter to become "a little lady". But the elder brother... the most frightening young man I've ever met.' She picked up a pencil and her fingers wound round it. She stood up quickly. 'Goodness, I don't know why I'm telling you all this.'

'Please don't worry,' I said and shook her hand. 'Roma Novans know how to keep a secret.'

3

Once through the security doors at the legation, I asked Furnia to send Captain Burnus to me. Well-built, fit and sharp-eyed, he was only in his late twenties – young for the head of Praetorian Guard detail at one of our most important legations. And his next promotion wouldn't be far off.

'It's bordering on the personal, Burnus,' I said, after recounting the episode at Marina's school. 'To be truthful, I did hesitate before calling you in, but I suppose you should be aware.'

'On the contrary, *nuncia*, it's essential for you to report such a threat. I appreciate it's only from a child, but one thing I've learnt since coming here is how close-knit these criminal families are.' He paused and brushed his beige uniform trousers with the tips of his fingers. 'I know with your PGSF service you are perfectly able to take care of yourself, but it's my job to protect the *nuncia* as representative of Roma Nova. In this case, you.'

'I know, Burnus. No need to give me a lecture.' This was always the problem with these high flyers – they thought they were superior to other mortals.

'I apologise, *nuncia*,' he said in a neutral tone, obviously miffed. He sat up straighter in the chair on the opposite side of my desk. 'I did not mean to appear insubordinate.'

'No, *I'm* sorry.' I smiled. 'And sorry that you have a headstrong principal to protect.'

'At least you are aware, *nuncia*. I suggest your daughter is accompanied by one of the guards as well as her nurse on her journey to and from school. They will vary their route. For the next few days we'll keep a watch in the area around the school. In the meantime, we'll run a background check on this Casely.'

After I'd given my assistant the job of coordinating the diplomatic families' day, I took a few minutes to think about Tom Carter.

Miklós had tracked him down once before for Harry during my previous posting as political officer in London. It had been eighteen months after that first incident at Harry's house. Afterwards, he'd said little apart from admitting Tom had been enmeshed in a very bad crowd. The two of them had been dropped off outside the legation in the most ramshackle van I'd ever seen. Its exhaust particles had ballooned in a black cloud in the frosty air. The driver with a toothy grin and felt hat had given a friendly wave before he'd ground the gears and the van lumbered off.

Miklós had been away for over a week that time. I was called down to the reception desk to verify him, as if he'd been an outsider. After a glacial look at the receptionist, I'd signed them both in. He and Tom traipsed in past the expressionless guard, Miklós supporting the slimmer figure with his arm round the boy's waist. Miklós had kissed me lightly on the lips then led Tom to the lift up to our apartment on the third floor. I was called in by the *nuncia* an hour later to explain myself.

'Your companion can't treat the legation as a way station for any dropout he chooses to take under his wing. Please have him remove the young man.'

'With respect, *nuncia*, that young man was falling over with exhaustion and ill. I've asked the doctor to take a look at him.'

'Mars alive! You go too far, Mitela,' she growled. Her voice wasn't just gravelly; it sounded as if it could cut marble. 'The legation *medicus* is solely for the use of the staff and their families, as you know well.'

'I'll reimburse the doctor's fee to the legation,' I replied in an equally cold voice.

She waved her hand impatiently. 'That's not the point.'

'I'm sure Assistant Secretary Carter at the British Foreign Ministry will be pleased to collect his son tomorrow,' I said, 'if the boy can be moved without worsening his condition.'

'He's Carter's son?' He voice had softened by half a tone to medium gravel. 'Very well, he can stay until he's fit to be moved. Keep me informed.'

That was five years ago. She'd retired from the diplomatic service now and taken her attitude with her into the commercial world. But I wondered if Miklós would be returning this time with Tom in the same exhausted and ill state as before. If he did, this time I would be having a stronger word with Harry.

I loved Miklós – heart, soul and mind – but gods, he was so unpredictable. Not even a telephone call to say where he was. I sighed. But without him my life would be desolate.

Two days later in the afternoon, Burnus knocked on my door and, once seated, handed me two sheets of paper stapled together.

'Casely. He's a really choice item and from a line of petty criminals,' he said. 'His father and uncle were in and out of prison for extortion, passing illegal currency and robbery. The uncle was accused of murder, but the state's witness vanished inexplicably.'

'Ah,' I said. 'One of those.'

'Yes, and it's archived now as a cold case.' He glanced at his papers. 'Casely's mother was a rough sort from the East End, anecdotally running a numbers racket, but nothing proved,' he continued. 'The father's second wife, Linda's mother, twenty years younger than her husband, seems to have come from a middle-class background. Father was a manager in the railway company, mother a teacher at the local school. And by the time he met her Casely senior had a mansion in Walthamstow and was on the local golf club committee.'

'This is fast work, Burnus.' I glanced at the second sheet. A London police report. No, a copy. 'How on earth did you get this?'

He said nothing, but looked at me gravely.

'Ah, no, don't tell me, then I can deny it when I get a complaint from the British police.' The sheet, mostly a table, charted John Casely's activities from theft from a newsagent's at age six, through fighting, bullying, burglary to armed robbery. No fatalities, but people's nerves and confidence shattered forever.'

'Thank you, I think,' I said.

'There's no question of withdrawing the guard at the school for the rest of your time here, *nuncia*. It's the best way with these types of people. They understand a show of force. Besides,' he said with a half-smile, 'it'll be a nice little training exercise in urban surveillance for the troops.'

'Pour one for me, would you?'

I whipped round in my chair, nearly spilling my evening drink. Miklós. My heart thudded. Gods, he looked tired. His eye sockets showed a brown tinge and his mouth was downturned. He flung himself down on the sofa and wiped his fingers across his forehead. The flames from the fireplace warmed my sitting room efficiently, but he shivered nonetheless.

He took a sip from the glass of French brandy I handed him, then drank the rest in one swallow. I fetched him another. He took a measured sip then leaned back and closed his eyes. He took several deep breaths to calm himself. I'd rarely seen him so agitated. After a couple of minutes, he opened his eyes.

'I'm sorry, *drágám*, but I haven't slept properly for two days. Do you mind if I go to bed now? I'll tell you everything in the morning. The main thing is I've failed. I'm so sorry.'

A flicker of anger passed through his eyes which tightened. Then he closed them again. I took his hand and kissed it. He heaved himself up as if he had the weight of an old time legionary marching yoke on his shoulders. In the bedroom, he peeled his clothes off and fell into the bed. I drew the covers over him and kissed his forehead. He was asleep almost instantly. I closed the door carefully and went back to the fireside.

He woke just after six the next morning as I was pulling on my tracksuit and running shoes. Running nearly every morning with the Praetorians kept the fat of diplomatic life off. It also woke me up properly for the day.

'Don't go,' he said and reached out for my hand. Now he only looked tired instead of exhausted. I lay down on the bed beside him.

'What happened, Miklós?'

'I thought I had a lead, but it petered out. One of the stable lads, Maury, has a brother who had trouble with the police when he was younger. He'd been a lookout for a drug dealer and went to a tough prison for a few months.' He snorted. 'Well, all prisons must be tough. But anyway, Maury took me to a pub east of here, the other side of the city wall, down near the docks, where we met his brother, Davy. It was a dark, unfriendly place. And it smelt, not just of smoke and sweat, but of centuries of dirt and graft.

'Maury took me to a corner and introduced me to Davy. He wouldn't let me go to the bar and buy drinks. He said I looked and sounded too foreign. They don't like foreigners – they throw them into the street and give them "a good hiding".' He glanced at me. 'A beating, I presumed?'

'Yes. Sounds charming. Go on.'

'Davy was very reluctant to say anything, but I gave him fifty pounds. You should have seen his eyes. It was like flicking a switch.'

'Shouldn't you have paid him *after* getting information?'

'No, with people like Davy once they have been given an advance, they feel an obligation, not least to themselves, to try to extract even more cash from the punter.'

'Ha! Anything useful?'

'I gave him Tom's first name and a detailed description and suggested he could be sleeping rough, drinking and doing some small con tricks or thieving. Davy tried not to react, but he blinked hard. Maury told him to tell us everything, but Davy clammed up.'

'Tom's very distinctive with that strong widow's peak Harry gave him. And his mother's blond hair.'

'Oh, Davy knew him. I'm sure of that, but he wouldn't answer anything more. When he left, I followed him round for a bit. He lives in an old terraced house – one of those red-brick jobs with passageways in the middle to a back alleyway. Nothing happened for hours, just some shouting and then television noise. He surfaced about eleven the next morning and I followed him to a bookies, then the same pub.'

'That's your fifty gone.'

'Probably. But half an hour after Davy had entered the pub, a tall thin figure, collar up, a Dutch bargee hat on his head, followed him in.' Miklós looked away and studied the ceiling for a few seconds. 'I couldn't swear to it, and it was raining hard, but it may have been Tom.'

'Gods! What did you do?'

'I crossed over to the corner entrance, turned the handle to push the door open, then somebody thumped me on the head. I went out cold. I woke up in the middle of the A12 with a head full of pain and the noise of heavy rumbling. A lorry was speeding towards me. God knows how I wasn't run over.'

My hand flew to my mouth. I pulled the covers back. I hadn't seen the bruising last night, just the exhaustion in his face. I reached towards the handset by the bed to call the doctor. Miklós grabbed my wrist.

'No, it's okay. Let me finish. I managed to stagger to the edge of the road, bent over it and was sick. My eyes were blurry, but I could see I was on a bridge, a flyover near the bank of a small dirty river. A voice called up, somehow cutting through a gap in the traffic. I slumped down at the edge. My head was spinning. The next thing I knew, I was being lifted into a car, and soft words were assuring me I was safe. I woke in a small room. A man was sitting in an old chair, reading. When he came over, I saw from his collar and cross he was a priest.'

'Where the hell were you?'

'Not there, it seems.' He smiled. 'I couldn't remember anything – not my name, what had happened or anything. He took me to a hospital. I remember laying down on a hard surface – probably an X-ray table. After that, I woke up in the priest's house again. The headache was less. Then I remembered everything. To say I felt like shit was an understatement. I got out of bed and found the kitchen for some food. And more water. The priest wasn't there.'

'Why didn't you phone me? I would have come immediately.'

'There was no telephone. Maybe he had one in the office in his church. But I just wanted to get out. Whoever dropped me could come back and I didn't want the priest to get into trouble, so I started walking.'

'Couldn't you find a phone box?'

'They'd taken all my money as well as my leather jacket. I did find two boxes on my way here, but both were vandalised. I gave up. It took me about four hours to get here. I found a drink on the way from a charity caravan giving out tea and coffee to the homeless.'

'Oh, gods.' I stretched out and cradled him in my arms, almost not breathing in my joy to have him back. I didn't care what he said, I would get the doctor to check him over. I was the *nuncia* this time and nobody could stop me. By the time I slipped carefully out of his arms, he was dozing again. And I was raging.

4

I hadn't calmed down completely by the time I left the legation just after eight, but walking to school with Marina was such a joy that the rest of my anger dispersed. Although weak, the autumn sunlight bounced golden lights off Marina's hair. She clasped my hand firmly, but half danced as we made our way along the path across the green in front of the school. Furnia walked more soberly a few paces behind. Inside, the hubbub of high-pitched excited voices only dimmed when the teacher took the register. Twenty minutes later, a crocodile of sixteen girls left the front door, Marina clasping her new friend Susanne's hand instead of mine. We parents and helpers were assigned to the rear.

Marina turned and glanced at me once, and waved. I waved back. I might have had to put off two meetings, situation report reading and drafting, but nothing was more important than spending this day with my daughter.

The London Museum was built to the west of the wall and incorporated remains of some old Roman houses. The mosaics were provincial but would have been adequate for the time. But then Roma Nova had also been founded near a provincial capital, so who was I to talk?

A young guide, earnest and a little nervous, greeted us. He kept pushing his spectacles back up his nose; the large glass lenses must have been too heavy for his skinny face. After a quick tour and demonstrations of children's costumes and reconstructions of a typical day for children in various centuries, the girls were allowed to wander round with their notebooks and pencils; some took photos with instant pocket cameras. Marina beckoned me into the Roman gallery and I crouched down to help her translate some of the inscriptions for her friends. She threw her arms around my neck while her friends stood round in a circle.

'Are you a real Roman, then?' one of the girls asked, her eyes wide.

'I am indeed, but a modern one,' I replied and returned her smile.

After their picnic lunch, they were organised into teams to play ancient games. The guide told Marina's group that although the museum considered they had all the pieces, they weren't exactly sure how one of the Roman games was played. Before I could say anything, she piped up.

'I've been playing these games since I was six. I know how they go. Any Roma Novan does.'

I had to clamp my lips together to prevent myself from laughing. Marina turned her back on the guide and continued instructing the other children. She looked the happiest I'd seen her since we'd arrived in the UK.

All of them except the delinquent girl, Linda Casely, joined in. She sucked the end of a lock of hair and stared at the girls chattering and shouting when they scored a point. Strangely, she didn't look unhappy, just smug. What on earth was going on in her head? I felt sorry for her standing apart and was about to go over and encourage her to join in, but at that moment the teacher clapped her hands.

'Pack up your things. We'll be leaving to go back to school in ten minutes. Those who need the lavatory, please go now to the ladies'.' She eyed Susanne's mother, Anna, and me. 'Perhaps some of the mothers would supervise them.'

Given our orders, we ushered the half-dozen girls including Marina and Linda Casely down the corridor. We waited outside as it was a small room; six lively girls would fill it. I smiled at Anna, who returned it with a chuckle. I was delighted that Marina's new friend had such an intelligent mother with a good sense of humour. Perhaps I had found a new friend as well.

Then the chatting and laughing stopped. I turned towards the door. What were they up to in there? A child screamed. Not excitement. Terror. I shoved the door open. Marina, Susanne and another girl were frozen still, staring at a man pointing an old-fashioned revolver at them. At his side, Linda was smirking.

I lunged forward, grabbed the revolver and punched the man in the face. He crumpled into a heap, cursing through his hands grasping his broken nose. Furnia barged in behind me. She dropped to her knees, turned him onto his front and had secured his wrists with narrow duct tape before I had time to take another breath.

Not a sound. Then one of the girls whimpered. Then another.

'It's safe. You're all safe,' I said, glancing down at each one in turn. 'Now, take three big breaths each.'

Six pairs of eyes stared up at me, but they opened their mouths obediently. The door opened a crack. Susanne's mother.

'Anna, can you take the other girls back to the teacher?'

'What's happened?' She stared around and shrank at the figure on the floor not entirely obscured by Furnia's figure. *'Herregud!'* Her hand flew to the base of her throat.

'There was an incident, but it's over. Finished. I'll catch up with you later.'

Anna looked at the girls then at me, anxiety in her eyes.

'It's over, Anna, but the girls need to leave. Now.'

Anna nodded, drew herself up and grabbed the door handle.

I gave my daughter an encouraging smile. 'Marina, look after everybody. I'll be with you in a moment.'

She nodded, her face solemn. She took Susanne's hand and followed Anna and the others out. I grabbed Linda Casely's wrist as she tried to leave. She squirmed, but I gripped her firmly. 'You're coming with me, miss, to see the headmistress.'

I turned to Furnia, then looked down at the figure on the floor, lashing out with his feet and cursing with words no child should hear. 'Take this piece of filth away with you round a corner out of public view. Radio Burnus and tell him to get the British police here ASAP, then go with them to make a statement. I'll follow.'

'I assure you, Miss Buckley, the girls are all safe. The City Police arrived and took the man and his handgun away. My staff and I handled the situation with maximum discretion so that it didn't develop into a graver incident.'

'Has the man been identified?' she said. The poor woman looked as if she'd been drinking garum fish sauce for a week.

'Not formally,' I replied, 'but it seems he is Linda Casely's brother. She called him "John" and called after him when my escort took him away. The civil police have asked me to make a statement and look through their book of known criminals. I insisted on escorting the teacher and girls back and coming to see you first.' I leant back in my chair and looked up at the ceiling, then back at her worried face. 'What you do about Linda is obviously your decision, but Marina will not be attending school while she is still here.'

Back at the legation, I wasn't surprised to see Miklós already talking to Marina. He was holding her hand and speaking softly to her as he would to a nervous foal. She was smiling up at him. My heart clenched. He was a good father to her, far better than her own natural one had ever been. If only our child together had survived, not lying in a tiny urn in the family tomb at home, thanks to that bastard Caius Tellus. He, at least, was rotting in a Prussian jail.

Both heads turned as I closed the door.

'Mama.' Marina held out her free hand. I took it and folded her into my arms. Miklós nodded to me over her head. I couldn't say anything for a minute or two. I just held the thin body of my child close to my heart.

'It's all right, Mama. I'm well,' she said her voice muffled by my jacket. I leant back. 'You were there. I knew you would look after me. The others were frightened, but I told them to be brave. Their screams gave me a headache.'

I laughed, then she giggled back.

'I've told Miss Buckley you'll be missing school for a few days,' I said.

'Oh, good,' Marina said, and beamed up at me.

'I'll be back for supper, but I have to go and give the police a statement.' I paused. 'Do you think you could write everything out that *you* saw?'

'Aurelia,' Miklós almost growled. 'You can't ask a child of eleven to make a witness statement. She was terrified. She won't remember anything. She needs to forget it and rest.'

We both stared at him and he looked from Marina, then slowly back at me.

'Of course I remember everything, Miklós,' Marina answered in a haughty voice. 'I'm not stupid. I was scared, but I know what I saw. I shall do that now.'

He threw his hands up. 'I might have known it. Romans. Pah!'

'Will they put that man in prison, Mama?' Marina asked, ignoring him.

'I certainly hope so.'

Downstairs, the legal *consultor* himself was waiting for me. Portly, but exuding that confidence possessed by cynical lawyers in sharp suiting, he greeted me.

'*Salve*, Rubrius. I am honoured having the chief lawyer turn out for me. I thought you were a trade contract expert.' I raised one eyebrow.

'Ah, *nuncia*, I have dabbled in many areas in my career. In my earlier years, I was a member of a chambers here in London that dealt almost exclusively in criminal cases. It's my honour to represent you.'

'Very well, but I can't think it will be very complex... just a statement.'

'It's the simple things that can trip us up most effectively.'

At the police station, a male detective sergeant led us into an interview room where another plainclothes officer sat behind a grey-topped utility table. The second man looked as if he'd just left school. I recited an account of events, and although they recorded everything, the younger one scribbled away. At the end I folded my hands in my lap and waited.

'What made you leap into action, Mrs Mitela? Why didn't you back away and call the police?' The sergeant frowned at me.

'And leave the children at the mercy of a man pointing a gun at them?'

'That was a highly risky gesture that could have ended in you being shot and several children injured or killed.'

The gods spare me!

'Sergeant, it was no risk to me. I knew if I acted quickly, I could disarm the man before he could even react to my intervention.'

'Really?' He didn't quite sneer. 'What makes you think you're Rambo?'

'That was uncalled for, sergeant,' Rubrius interrupted.

I laid my palm on the lawyer's sleeve and shook my head.

'Until a few years ago, I was a soldier, specifically the Praetorian Guard Special Forces. I trust you understand the term 'special forces'? I led many operations, including hostage and urban support. One never forgets these things, especially when you've done them for over ten years. Disarming a young hooligan frightening children in a ladies' lavatory was hardly challenging.'

'Hm. I'll have to check what you're saying.'

Rubrius took a sharp breath in.

'I assure you, sergeant, Roma Novans do not lie,' I snapped. 'Please also remember I am a fully accredited diplomat.'

'Your friend who held the suspect could be seen as detaining him illegally.'

'Friend? Oh, you mean *Optio* Furnia? She is another Praetorian, a member of our diplomatic protection detail. She was acting under my orders.'

'Red herring, sergeant,' Rubrius added. 'An "any person" arrest is perfectly permissible of anyone who is in the act of committing an offence – for instance, possession of a weapon in a public place. As there was no police officer present and there was considerable risk of the person absconding before an officer could assume responsibility for him, I would say that my client and *Optio* Furnia acted with impeccable speed and effectiveness. Now do you have any further questions, or can the ambassador sign her statement?'

Due to paperwork and meetings the next day, I was stuck at my desk with no prospect of joining Miklós and Marina for lunch. Halfway through the afternoon when I was going through next week's schedule with my assistant, an *optio* knocked at my door.

'The signals officer's compliments, *nuncia*, but there's a request from the foreign ministry for a one-to-one in fifteen minutes' time.'

'Can you ask them to put it back for half an hour, please?'

She glanced around as if trying to find her words.

'It's from Tertullius Plico, the imperial secretary, ma'am, and he was, er, insistent.'

'I see.' And he would have been a great deal less diplomatic than 'insistent'. 'Very well,' I said. 'Confirm the session. I'll be there shortly.'

Ten minutes later, I pressed the code pad by the signals office door and entered. Apart from a civilian typist, the staff consisted entirely of beige-and-black-uniformed military. The automated tapping of teleprinters and the hum of radio transmitter and receiver sets filled the room. White paper tape perforated in Murray code spilled from the teleprinters into catching bins. The duty signals officer greeted me and ushered me into one of the soundproofed booths where I set the headphones on my head and waited, watching the blank screen. The outgoing signal warbled briefly with the incoming, synched and the connection was established. As his image stabilised, I saw Plico was smiling. Worrying.

'*Salve*, Tertullius Plico. How's the weather in Roma Nova?'

'Oh, please!' he huffed. 'You're not at one of your parties now trying to talk to some half-witted diplomat.'

'Aren't you the cheerful one?'

'You will be if you give me a chance to speak.'

'What do you mean?'

'You're relieved as from next Wednesday. The new permanent *nuncio*, Publius Gracilis, has been appointed. He'll be with you Sunday to start handover. After that, you can come home.'

'Oh.'

'What? I thought you'd be leaping around for joy.'

'No, no. That's good news. It's just that I've just set up some personal stuff and I'd rather not cancel.'

'Well, you can take some of your leave – we won't charge you rent.'

'Thanks very much,' I said as sarcastically as I could. 'So generous.'

'Aren't I just?' He grinned. 'More seriously, I've got an intelligence job that needs somebody with your international experience to lead it.'

'Oh?' I tried not to sound too interested. 'Do tell.'

'Certainly not. You come home first.'

'Spoilsport.'

'Live with it.' He glanced at his watch. 'Meeting with the imperatrix. Must go.'

'Give her my love.'

'Humph. Right, get Gracilis up to speed, then let him get on with his job. I'll expect you back in the office in ten days from now.'

'I'm not sure that will be enough time for me to finish here.'

'What's so important? Have you got a one-to-one with the king scheduled?'

'Don't be ridiculous!'

'Then what?' He frowned.

'Nothing, just everyday stuff that I've already committed to on a personal level.'

Plico looked at me, searching my face.

'Why do I think you're up to something?'

'Ten days? That's impossible.' Miklós said. He stared at me out of a less exhausted face. At least the vivid purple of the bruising had faded to a dirty yellow. Weak sun fell through the windows of the residence sitting room, intent on fading the edges of the burnt orange velvet curtains.

'It's okay,' I said. 'I'll go back first – you follow when you're ready.'

'Plico thinks he rules the world, you included. Tell him to lose himself in the forum traffic.'

'I can't, darling. He's my boss.'

'You can walk out any time you want. You've got a full-time role as a senator, plus your wider family and running the businesses without this diplo stuff. And Justina will be pleased to see you back. She'll probably put you on her council in the next year or so.'

'Unlikely. I'm too young.'

'Young, yes, but you're the head of the Twelve Families.' He smiled at me, his eyes glistening. 'Care to make a bet?'

'No thanks. I wouldn't want to take your money.'

'Sometimes, Aurelia, underneath you're too unsure of yourself for your own good.'

'No, it's that I don't want to let people down.'

'You do too much already.'

'Perhaps, but I want to be useful.' I looked up at him and grinned.

'Besides, I love all the intrigue. I could do with a little more action, though.'

At which point, Miklós stood, pulled me up from my chair into his arms and kissed me hard, passionately and purposefully. He laughed as he slid the zip of my day dress down. It dropped to the floor in a heap of blue wool.

He took my hand in his warm one and led me to the bedroom where he eased me down onto the bed. His lips on my eyelids, my earlobe, my jawline. I had his shirt off within seconds and ran my hands over his chest, only touching the bruises lightly. He didn't even flinch.

That warm, rich masculine scent, so heady. I bent and kissed his lips and removed the rest of his clothes. I shed my silk slip and lingerie. Our skins touched head to foot and, passionately, we loved each other.

5

After breakfast the next day, Miklós said he was heading east to find the priest who had helped him.

'The doctor has cleared me—'

'Subject to you taking his pills.' I looked at him sternly, then smiled, remembering the previous night.

'Don't fuss, woman.'

'I'm not fussing, merely reminding you that you would be wiser to take the pills.'

'Yes, Miklós,' a high voice piped up. 'If the doctor and Mama say you must take them, then you must.'

He groaned and looked at the small plastic tub Marina was pointing to.

'Very well, but only because you Roman women won't leave me in peace if I don't.'

She gave him a broad smile, then jumped up, kissed him on the cheek, then ran off in the direction of the nursery.

'You'll think I'm fussing again if I ask you to be careful,' I said when Marina was out of earshot.

'I know you mean well, Aurelia. Don't worry, Burnus is coming with me. He said he could do with stretching his legs. Besides, he's sharp and may see something I don't.'

· · ·

I spent the rest of the day preparing for the handover. The steward and housekeeper would arrange our packing and temporary accommodation for Gracilis until we vacated the official residence flat. He was a single man and when I'd talked on the phone with him he'd seemed perfectly content with that.

I would fly back to Roma Nova on Thursday with Marina and settle her at the palace nursery with Justina's daughter's children, Julian and Silvia. She knew them well; she and Aemilia would soon be back in their routine.

Then I'd come back to London and with Miklós's help keep my promise to Harry Carter.

'Gracilis seems a smooth operator. He'll do well here,' Miklós commented a few days later as we updated our London travel passes at the kiosk. I slipped my credit card back in my inner pocket. It was a time-limited one; where we were going, I had to assume we might be robbed and come out only with our skins intact. We shuffled onto the escalator plunging down into the metro system.

'He and Harry seemed to take to each other,' I replied. 'And he'll be able to get right inside British inner circles if he joins a few clubs.' Ones I'd automatically been excluded from as a woman. I yawned.

'Are you okay to come on this trip?' Miklós said. I'd only returned from taking Marina back to Roma Nova the day before.

'Of course.' I grinned at him. 'Well, I wouldn't say no to another cup of coffee, however revolting. I'll get one the other end.'

We said nothing as we travelled east in the clanking carriages smelling of sweat, dirt and rubber. All the other passengers read their newspapers or books; one woman was knitting, some sat with their eyes closed, but I didn't think it was in meditation. A youngster was listening to something on his portable cassette player. I wondered idly if such things would ever become popular. But nobody risked talking.

Four stations along, we surfaced. Five minutes later we left the train as it continued east. We were the only passengers who stepped off at this point. Paint peeled off the fascia boards overhead and the concrete surface of the platform was cracked and holed. I pulled my scruffy parka in closer to my body against the cold breeze as we made for the metal-edged steps. I fished a hand-knitted green hat out of my pocket, twisted my hair up and smoothed the hat over my head.

It was only just gone eleven in the morning, but the low cloud gave the impression it was five or six in the afternoon.

'The pub's about half a kilometre south-east.' Miklós nodded to the exit.

'You and Burnus didn't find out anything more from the priest when you saw him again the other day?'

'Nothing. He looked at me solemnly like all priests do and said he'd been worried about me. But the important thing was that none of the ungodly visited him afterwards. They must have thought I'd been finished off in the traffic.'

I grasped his arm.

'Thank the gods you weren't!'

We continued along the terraced Victorian streets; some houses were well kept, but most were verging on the shabby. One or two little shops, dimly lit, were trading, but there were twice as many closed ones. The streets narrowed and the buildings became higher and dirtier. Cobbles shone through a thin layer of tarmac.

'Gods, it's like stepping back in time.' I could hardly believe we were in the capital of one of the world's strongest economies. 'Why on earth hasn't this part been redeveloped under the Peabody Plan?'

'I don't know. It didn't strike me as odd at the time.' He shrugged. 'All cities have slum areas.'

'Maybe, but this is like a time-slip island. The gods know what the water and electricity are like inside. I'll have a word with Harry to get an introduction to their urban development people and —'

'You aren't the *nuncia* now, Aurelia. They'll tell you to mind your own business.'

'This is everyone's business. I wonder who owns these streets...' Then it hit me. 'Ah. I see. Landlords, probably greasing the local planners' paws.' There were major trials of corrupt local government officers running in two northern English cities at present. Unlikely to be any different in the capital. 'Okay, let's get on.' I slumped and altered my walk to a more shambling style. We were both dressed in worn clothes and boots. Miklós had clipped his hair a centimetre and brushed it hard back. I glanced at my watch.

'Okay, it's five to twelve,' I said. 'The pub will open any minute.

Let's walk on a bit and look as if we're vaguely interested in renting a place.'

We walked slowly round the block of scruffy terraced houses. I glimpsed dull-coloured clothes hanging on clothes lines secured by old wooden posts leaning precariously. Some of the backyards had dilapidated privies, old tyres and rubble. Incredibly depressing. Back in the pub road, two small children were sitting on the kerb, fingers in the gutter. They looked up at us, assessed us, then ignored us.

'Gods, this place is a scandal,' I whispered.

'No different from slums in some of the Russian cities.'

'But that's the point. It shouldn't be like it here.'

He said nothing but pointed at the half-glazed pub door. The glass was frosted, but I could see a yellow orange light inside.

'Ready?' Miklós said.

I took a deep breath, glanced round for any watchers, then nodded. He pushed the door open and I followed him into the Victorian age. Two men by a half-frosted window were smoking. Another, at the bar. Miklós nodded me in the direction of one of two tables in a corner, where I sat on the padded bench and waited obediently. It was half-partitioned off with dark wood uprights. He came back with a pint for him and a half for me.

'How very quaint,' I whispered after I'd taken a sip.

'You'd look odd as a woman swigging a pint,' he murmured as he leant back against the padded plastic.

'Now we wait,' I said. He picked up a sports newspaper from the neighbouring table and studied the racing form. I had to content myself with yesterday's ranting tabloid. Just over half an hour later, Miklós nudged me as a small wiry man entered. He looked around carefully and walked over to the bar. He sat down on the back bench at the table next to ours, glanced sideways at me, then sipped his beer. After a minute, Miklós laid the newspaper down and looked unsmilingly at the man.

'Hello, Davy.'

The small man choked, looked around for help, tried to stand but Miklós grabbed the back of his waist belt and heaved him back down. The barman looked over, but Miklós shook his head at him. The man went back to polishing glasses.

'We need to have a little chat, Davy.' Miklós shuffled up and transferred his newspaper to Davy's table. 'Let's study the form together.' His voice was hard.

'I didn't 'ave nothin' to do with what happened to you,' Davy said.

'And what do you think happened to me?' Miklós stared hard.

Davy looked down at his drink and shrugged, the shoulder nearest Miklós higher than the other.

'And who gave them the signal about me?'

'I don't know nothin' about that.'

'Mind-reading is only for the fairground. It must have been you.'

'I didn't do nothin'.'

'No, you didn't and that's the point. So what did Tom have to say when he met you here in the pub?'

'Don't know who you're talking about.'

'I'm not a fool, Davy. I saw Tom Carter walk in through that door. Tell me what he said to you.'

Davy took a gulp of his beer.

'We can protect you, you know,' Miklós said in a softer tone.

Davy looked at him with pure disbelief all over his face. He snorted.

'Not against them, you can't.'

Miklós shifted on the slippery bench and opened his mouth to say something, but the outside door at the corner swung open. A tall figure in a raincoat, greasy hair receding but the ends touching a grey shirt collar at the back, stood looking round. He stopped for scarcely a second at Davy, then moved on. He blinked when he saw Miklós, but looked away, then bought a packet of cigarettes at the bar. While he was getting his change, Miklós said to Davy, 'Thanks Davy, you've been really helpful.' The man looked over at Davy with hard grey eyes, then turned and left.

Davy looked horrified and tried to get up, but Miklós grasped his arm. I pulled myself up and slouched as if towards the ladies', but slipped out the side door, pulling my hat off as I went through.

Out in the street, I shook my head so my hair fell down and half hid my face. Then I peered around and saw the raincoated man yank open a red telephone box. I walked past. Hades, if only I had one of those scanners Numerus had used in Berlin, I could have listened in.

I stared up the street and waited. Something big and black with loud wings flew towards me. Pluto in Tartarus. A bloody raven. That was all we needed. It settled on top of the phone box and fixed its yellow eye on me. I turned away. Apollo's black messenger could take a run and jump, preferably over the Styx. I shivered, though.

As he left the box two minutes later, the man walked in my direction. I turned and studied the dirty window of a newsagent's shop. The man strode past, glanced back at me then opened the door of a yellow-ochre coloured saloon and drove off.

I pushed my hair back under my hat and ambled back into the pub, and went back to the pub. No Davy.

'He tore out of the other door like a rabbit smelling the stewpot,' Miklós said.

'Well, Raincoat Man made a phone call, then drove off.'

'I wondered why you were back so quickly.'

'At least I've got the number in the phone box and the car registration.'

'Harry Carter, please,' I said to the switchboard operator. As we'd pre-arranged, I pretended to be his cousin Margaret to get past his secretary.

'Darling,' I said in my best plummy British accent. 'Do say you can come out for afternoon tea.'

'Lovely to hear from you, Mags. Usual place?'

'I'll save you a seat.'

Fifteen minutes later, Miklós, Harry and I huddled in the back of a tiny café near Charing Cross station which specialised in weak tea and factory-made cakes. I tore off a leaf from my spiral bound notebook and handed it to Harry.

'Can you trace this car registration and also find out the number of the phone, and its owner, that the raincoated man was calling from the phone box? And their address?'

'Steady on, Aurelia,' Harry said in a low voice. 'You can't think I have instant access to these lists. Besides, we can't trace number somebody calls unless we're intercepting them already.'

'Hades.'

'Look, I'll get somebody to check the three LVLOs for London for the car.'

'LVLO?'

'Local vehicle licensing offices.'

'You don't have a central registry?' I said. 'Computerised records?'

'Yes, and it's all white coats and wash until you're sterile to get in there, let alone waiting a week for an access time. Then they have to run a special program and they won't let you breathe on their precious machines. But we'll be able to walk in to the LVLOs and get all the details from the local records files. Instantly.' He parked the note in the pocket inside his suit jacket, then took another forkful of the tasteless sponge cake with the thinnest line of jam I'd ever seen. 'I don't suppose you've made any other progress?'

Miklós sat up and leant forward. The noise in the little café would have drowned his voice out anyway. 'Not unless you count being beaten up and left to die in the middle of the highway,' he murmured and looked Harry direct in the eye.

'WHAT?' Harry blurted out. His face froze in shock. His fork dropped onto his plate with a crash. People around us stared at him. 'What the hell happened?' he continued in a quieter voice. Miklós gave him a rundown.

'We don't know for certain it was Tom that Miklós saw on that first trip to the pub,' I added. 'But we have to add it into the mix.'

Harry swallowed.

'I can't let you and Miklós get into this kind of danger. This has gone beyond asking friends to do a favour.'

I laid my hand on his forearm.

'No, Harry, I promised you. And attacking Miklós was their mistake. It now becomes my business. Just find me that car and its driver. Then we'll go hunting.'

6

'Are you going to sell the stud when we move back to Roma Nova permanently?' Miklós kept his eyes on the road, but shifted in his seat as he changed gear.

'Gods, no. It's a good investment,' I replied. 'Besides, you love it!'

'You haven't bought me with it, you know.'

Juno, what did that mean?

'Miklós, I—'

'Silly, I was only teasing.' He glanced at me. 'But I don't need expensive gifts, Aurelia. I'm just happy to be with you.'

'But I love sharing what I have with you.'

'You don't need to. Just share your love with me.'

I didn't say anything for the next few miles as we sped up the motorway towards Cambridge. I'd never said as much to Miklós but something about the countryside round the stud spooked me. He'd fallen in love with it when we'd gone to view it before buying. He said it was true horse country. People had bred and raced here since ancient times, he was sure. He could feel it in his bones. Yes, and those same ancients had slaughtered my people in their tens of thousands during the rebellion in the first century. Maybe that was it. Perhaps some instinct in my genes smelt the blood. It was too open, too close to the wide, empty fenlands, too much open sky. Then it started to rain and wind blew across the flat, featureless landscape under a dark grey sky. I shivered despite the car's heater blasting out warmth.

I'd bought Thurswick Stud, a few miles from the Oldmarket Racecourse, several years ago as an investment. Breeding potential racehorses had seemed a good prospect, and with an experienced manager in place, it had worked out very well. We'd bred several Royal Ascot winners and a recent Derby winner, with a good number of yearlings and two-year-olds looking hopeful for the future.

As we parked the hire car in the yard today, I was impressed by how neat and tidy it was. As we walked round, that impression was reinforced. Lambert, the manager, had come with top level recommendations; they were proving more than true. The stable hands were going about their duties of mucking out, filling water buckets, refilling hay nets and such, with cheerful expressions. The horses themselves, some dozing, but most looking with pricked ears and interest over their stable doors towards us as we strolled along the first row of loose boxes, looked fit, well and content. I smiled as several of them whickered a greeting to Miklós as he put his hand out to stroke a muzzle or pull affectionately at an ear.

After a few minutes enjoying himself, Miklós took in a long breath, nodded at me and went to look for Maury, Davy's more respectable brother. The rain had stopped at last and I took Lambert back outside to talk business strategy. I kept a light touch; this was Miklós's project. But as we made our way across the yard, the sound of raised voices rang out. Miklós's was one, the other was lighter in tone, but just as forceful. The stud manager looked at me, one eyebrow raised.

'I'll take it from here, Mr Lambert,' I said. 'I think it may be personal rather than professional.' He hesitated, then nodded. I waited until he was back near the office door before I entered the stable block. Leather, live animal and damp straw smells hit me. Miklós's mouth was set in a straight line, his arms crossed and shoulders tight. He was staring down at Maury who was waving a fist at him.

'What in Hades is going on here? We can hear your voices from the other side of the yard,' I hissed.

Maury twisted his head round to face me.

'It's him.' He jabbed a finger at Miklós. 'He's going to kill my brother.'

'What?' I said. 'Don't be ridiculous.'

'Davy called me an hour ago.' He glared at Miklós. 'You was going to treat him okay. At least I thought so when you gave him that fifty. He was proper scared and—'

'Calm down, Maury,' I broke in. 'Nobody is going to kill anybody. In fact, Miklós offered to protect him if he told us what he knew.'

'You're lying. I believe my brother first.'

I seized his jacket collar and pulled. Even in the gloom, I saw the fright in his eyes.

'Now listen to me, Maury. You don't accuse me of lying. Roma Novans don't need to. Your toerag brother led Miklós into a trap where they almost killed him.'

'What do you mean?'

'Oh, didn't he give you that detail?' I released him and wiped my hand on my coat. He coughed, then looked at me sullenly. 'What exactly did your brother say?'

'That you was after Tom Carter and would kill anybody in your way. We all know what you Romans are like. Tough as hell.' He pointed at Miklós. 'He's a bit better, not much, mind.'

'I know Davy's your brother, Maury, but he's distorted everything. Either he's so frightened of the people he's associated with or he's deep in with them. Either way, I suggest you keep away from him for a while.'

We found a little pub on the outskirts of Cambridge which had rooms. Miklós wouldn't admit it, but he was still recovering from his attack and I didn't want to drive back this late. We'd have another talk with Maury in the morning when he'd had time to digest what we'd said. Full of beef bourguignon and a surprisingly good red wine followed by French brandy, we collapsed under the frilly-edged duvet into the care of Morpheus.

A hard knocking on the door. I struggled awake. My watch said six-twenty. Faint light from a streetlight shone through the gap between the floral-patterned curtains.

'Hello?'

'Urgent message for you, madam,' the voice muffled by the door said. It sounded like the landlady from the previous night, Mrs Hicks, but you never knew.

I pulled on my shirt and slacks and, standing to the side of the frame, I opened the door a few centimetres. The smiling face from yesterday evening had disappeared. Instead, a hard expression reflected anxiety. She chewed her lip.

'I've got the police downstairs. For you.'

Hades. Now what?

'Give me five minutes.'

We traipsed downstairs, where the landlady had rallied enough to thrust mugs of tea into our hands. Two policemen rose from the table where we'd eaten yesterday evening. One young, but the other bulkier with white hair at his temples.

'Mrs Mitela?' He glanced at his pocket book. 'Mr Farkas?' His younger colleague half smirked. I glared at him and he looked away.

'Yes. How can we help you?'

'Did you speak to a man called Maurice Finer at the Thurswick Stud yesterday?'

'Yes, he's an employee there. I own it.' I studied the policeman's face. 'What's happened?'

'He's in hospital, badly beaten, and mentioned Mr Farkas here. According to the stud manager, a Mr Lambert, Finer and Mr Farkas were arguing loudly.'

Miklós took a step forward, but I raised my hand.

'When was this supposed to have happened?' I asked.

'Finer left for home about eight, then called for help about eleven. Where were you between those hours?'

'We left the stud at half seven, drove here, ate dinner here, then went to our room and slept.'

The policeman looked at the landlady who nodded.

'Very well. We'll need statements from all of you.'

'Of course,' I said. 'Can we visit him?'

'Not until we've investigated further.'

Mrs Hicks served us breakfast in complete silence, but it was well cooked and plentiful. The coffee was undrinkable. The woman hovered, fiddling with the pile of paper napkins, rearranging cutlery in a tray on the side and refilling plastic containers with breakfast cereals.

Miklós shook his head as I stood up when I'd finished, but I ignored him. I went up to the landlady.

'I'm sorry you had an unwelcome visit this morning, Mrs Hicks. I wouldn't have wished it on you for the world.'

She glanced up at me. I was surprised to see not worry or irritation, but real anxiety in her eyes.

'That's not it. It was that man in the bar last night. My Dan said he looked hard, like a fighter, but he was very controlled. He said he wanted to see you and your friend about buying Thurswick Stud.' She twisted a cloth between her fingers.

'Really? I wonder how he knew we were here?'

'I don't know, but I said you'd retired for the night. He said he'd come back to talk to you this morning.' She stopped pulling at the cloth. 'I hope he doesn't.'

'Please don't worry, Mrs Hicks. We'll deal with him if he does.' I glanced at my watch. 'We're not due at the police station to give our statements for an hour. Mr Farkas and I will go and sit in the lounge and see if he turns up. Perhaps you could bring us some tea there?'

She bustled through the swing door to the kitchen. I sat back at the table.

'If he's after us, I suppose he spotted the car,' I murmured to Miklós.

'Agreed. Then he must have been at the stud as well.'

Half an hour later, as we were reading the excuses for newspapers, Raincoat Man walked into the pub lounge. Our chintz-covered chairs were tucked away in the corner inside formed by the entrance porch so he didn't seem to have spotted us. He wore the same grey shirt and trousers under his dark raincoat. Then he turned round. Cold, hard eyes. Not on the same level as my old nemesis, Caius Tellus, but pitiless in the same way.

'Here it comes,' I muttered. Miklós laid his paper down and studied the man neutrally but unflinchingly as he covered the few steps to reach us. I smelt the spicy, almost brutal cologne before he slid into the spare chair at our table.

'This is nice,' he said and drew out and lit a cigarette.

'What can we do for you?' I said. He looked me over as if assessing merchandise.

'Nothing I want from you, love,' he said and turned away. He jabbed his cigarette at Miklós. 'Now, you, you keep away from what don't concern you. You had a nasty accident. You don't want a permanent one, do you?'

Miklós said nothing.

'Who are you working for?' I said.

Raincoat Man looked at me, then back at Miklós. 'You want to keep a lock on her mouth if I was you. You don't want her losing her tongue, do you? Or maybe you do.' He smiled. Not pleasantly. 'Let me know,' he continued almost genially. 'Happy to oblige.' He glanced at his watch. 'Must get on.' He stood, then walked out, whistling as he left. I twisted round and scanned the pub car park. There was the same car Raincoat Man had driven off in before. I went straight to the payphone by the door to the ladies' to call Harry. I had to know now who we were dealing with. I stared out of the window as the call connected. A raven had perched on the bench outside and shrieked into the wind.

7

'Why didn't you want to mention Raincoat Man to the scarabs?' Miklós asked as we drove to the southern outskirts of Cambridge after a boring hour at the local police station. I smiled at his use of the Roma Novan slang for the police.

'It wouldn't have helped. Harry didn't have the car registration details when I phoned so we still don't know who the owner is. As they're using it openly, I suspect it's owned rather than stolen. And if there *is* some connection to Tom, I'd rather tell Harry first.'

'Would you have told them if you'd known who he was?'

'Probably not.'

He said nothing but swung the car into the hospital car park and found a space at the end. He unbuckled his seat belt.

'No, you wait here,' I said. 'You're too distinctive.'

'And you're not remarkable?' His tone was sceptical.

'Not as much as you.' I removed my gold earrings, shook my hair out of its chignon and swapped my tailored jacket for the old parka I'd worn on our trip to the East End. It mostly hid my navy slacks. I wiped my dark lipstick off and tied a pair of trainers on my feet instead of my court shoes. The green knitted hat completed my transformation. Reaching over to the back seat I picked up the supermarket packet of grapes I'd bought when we'd filled up with petrol. 'Back soon,' I said as I shut the door behind me.

I took a deep breath of the fresh air before pushing the glazed door at the hospital entrance.

'Morning visiting hours finish in fifteen minutes,' the over made-up receptionist intoned, looking down her nose at my scruffy appearance.

'I just got some grapes for my cousin,' I mumbled. 'He came in last night. Had an accident.'

'Men's general, second floor,' she said and pointed at a stairwell containing an open lift cage in its centre. I traipsed up the metal-edged steps to a corridor with a lino floor. At the ward entrance I hesitated.

'Can I help you?' A woman in blue, wearing a white apron and cap, and an efficient air, stood in front of me. I lifted the packet of grapes.

'For Maury. He come in last night.'

'I'll make sure he gets them.' She held out her hand.

'Can I jus' see him? To tell my aunt he's okay?' I gave her my most pathetic look. She looked me up and down.

'Oh, very well, but he might be asleep. The doctor gave him a sedative and the effects haven't worn off completely. Third bed on the left.'

I nodded and shuffled up the ward. One of the other beds opposite had visitors, but there were none on the left. Maury's hand was outside the bedcovers and bandaged. His face was red and purple and a gash ran across one cheek.

As quietly as I could, I approached his bed, setting the grapes down on the bedside table. He stirred and I held the plastic beaker of water to his lips.

'Thanks,' he said. Then he opened his eyes, shut them, then half opened them. 'Oh, Gawd. It *is* you.' He took a quick breath, then grunted. 'You was right.' He turned his face away. 'I don't know what Davy's got mixed up with, but they're some real bastards.'

'What have the doctors said about you? Anything broken?'

'Nothing that won't get better, they say. I got another X-ray tomorrow.'

'Very well. You stay here as long as you need to, Maury, then you take sick leave until you're completely well. No struggling back to work. I'll talk to Mr Lambert.' I checked to see if anybody was looking or listening. 'I'm your cousin Grace, by the way.'

He frowned.

'I'm sure this is part of something much bigger, Maury. Mr Farkas and I are going to sort it out, but in our own way. Have you given a full statement to the police?'

'I was too out of it when they first come. They're coming back tomorrow. What do you want me to say?'

'Just tell them the truth about the attack. Nobody knows who did this to you. I'm going to do my best to find out, but privately. If they ask you about the argument with Mr Farkas, just say it was a professional difference.'

'Okay.'

'Did the person who attacked you ask you anything? Or tell you anything?'

'Just wanted to know if I was Davy's brother. And your names. But everybody knows you anyway, that you own the stud.' He tried to sit up and winced and dropped back. 'He said I was a warning to you and said you'd better listen good.'

'Oh, Maury, I'm so sorry.' I took his uninjured hand and gave it a gentle press.

'Don't worry, Grace,' he said, a little louder and pressed my hand in turn. The ward sister was two steps away. 'Tell Auntie Madge I'll soon be as right as rain.'

'So it *was* targeted after all, and at us,' Miklós said as we set off back down the motorway to London.

'Undoubtedly. We have to assume we were being watched. Odd.'

'Are you slipping, Aurelia?' He grinned.

I batted him on his arm with the back of my hand.

'I'm out of the game, I know, but I'm not that sloppy.' It was over seven years since I'd last served as a Praetorian Guard Special Forces officer and fiver since my last spying trip for Tertullius Plico, but you didn't lose all that expertise that quickly. Maybe I *had* relaxed a little as I thought I was just carrying out a temporary diplo job.

'We must make contact with Harry urgently to find out about that blasted car,' I said. 'Apart from the pub, that's our only lead.'

But an envelope was waiting for me at the legation.

'Harry Carter gave me this for you at our meeting earlier this morning, countess,' Gracilis, the new *nuncio*, said with a solemn expression on his face. In his slim hand was a cream envelope bearing my name and marked *Private and confidential. Eyes only.*

Upstairs in the residence, I tore it open.

Not much luck, I'm afraid. According to the records the car was sold for scrap two years ago by a John Casely. He's currently on bail for a firearms offence.

'Gods! Casely. How is he mixed up in all this?' I said.

'What else?' Miklós asked.

My man had them print out a photocopy of the surrendered V60 logbook. The address is genuine, an old garage, but it was condemned last year and demolished. Bit of a dead end, I'm afraid.

I've notified the police. The vehicle is probably unsafe and uninsured. Hopefully, they'll take it off the road and that will stop them.

Best wishes,

H

Miklós held his arms out as if trying to contain a wild horse, but I was too angry to move into them. I shook my head at him as I crushed Harry's note. My whole body trembled.

'Is he that naive? Or merely stupid?' I shouted. 'What in Tartarus is he thinking of, telling the damned police?' I stamped my foot. 'He's just destroyed our best lead.' I strode around the room in an aimless pattern, radiating like a Fury. Miklós caught me and pulled me to him. He tightened his grip on me.

'Shush, shush. Calm yourself,' he whispered in my ear. 'Stop for a moment. Just breathe.'

Gradually, I stopped trembling and relaxed against his strength and warmth. He released his arms a little and I brought my hand up to his face.

'Sorry,' I murmured.

'No, don't be. It's all right. It's normal. You're a passionate creature, Aurelia. You take it so personally.'

'But we're trying to find his wretched son for him, and he's just sabotaged us.'

'Yes, but he didn't do it on purpose to hinder us, but out of what he sees as public duty.' He smiled down at me. 'You of all people should understand that.'

'Humph.' I dropped into a chair and took several sips of the brandy he'd handed me. 'We'll go and check the address anyway, just in case.'

Swathed in bike leathers we almost flew along the clearway east on a two-wheeled extravaganza of chrome and noise. Clinging on to Miklós's waist, I had to admit that it wasn't the most pleasant experience of my life, but the bike was perfect for negotiating passages and alleyways so we could be sure we weren't being followed. We cruised along the street where the old garage had been, but only a couple of lock-ups and a few houses remained. Most had boarded up windows and weeds growing out of the gutters. At the corner was a dimly lit small shop with yellow cellophane-lined windows. Not that it looked as if much sun pierced the street.

'I'll go and buy a cola,' I said, swinging my leg over the seat. Miklós nodded and stayed astride the bike. I handed him my helmet and shook my hair out.

The doorbell on the frame gave a dull grunt as I entered the shop. A middle-aged man in a shirt with straining buttons squatted on a stool behind the counter. He was bending over, absorbed in his adult comic. After a full minute, he looked up.

'Yes?' he leered as looked me up and down. 'Can I help you, darlin'?'

I tugged open the glazed door of the fridge, which made a sucking noise as it reluctantly parted from the body, and took out a can.

'Perhaps.' I put a twenty pound note down on the counter but held on to one end. 'Didn't there used to be a garage just up the road?'

'There might have been,' he said then looked away. He shifted in his seat and farted.

'Might? Yes or no?' I said, trying to ignore the smell.

'Piss off. And I'll take that.' His fingers went to snatch the note but I brought my other fist down on the back of his hand. He yelped then swore.

'You bitch. I should clock you for that.'

'Try,' I replied, and looked down my nose at him. He said nothing, but nursed his hand. The noise of footsteps, a whining child and squeaky pram wheels came and went outside. I waited. The shopkeeper glanced up at me, resentment all over his face, but greedy eyes on the twenty.

'Who wants to know, anyway?'

'I do.' I waved the note back. 'This could still be yours. But if you don't tell me, I'm not paying.' I picked up the cold can and walked towards the door.

'Wait.'

'Yes?'

'There was. Pulled down about a year ago.'

'Who owned it?'

'You don't want to know.'

I walked back to the counter and leaned across it, millimetres from his greasy face. He jerked his head back, a surprised look on his face.

'Don't tell me what I want,' I growled at him. 'Now, who owned it?'

'One of the local families.'

'Name names.'

He looked at the door, pulled his lips together. I laid the twenty pound note on the counter between us.

'It belonged to old man Casely, but he's gone from here. They say his son sold it, but I dunno more than that.'

'And that's it, Harry,' I reported. 'I think you must get your police involved now.' I'd settled into the easy chair by the telephone table in the residency sitting room. Half-packed boxes surrounded me and the torn-off printout of Plico's urgent telex curled on the table.

Now that we'd discovered the connection to Casely, it wasn't quite so bad that Harry had already informed the police about the car. 'Casely's hearing for the firearm offence must come to court soon,' I continued. 'I've made a statement, as has *Optio* Furnia, so he must be convicted for that.' I stared out of the window at the rain giving the lamps on the streetlights pale yellow halos.

'Hopefully,' Harry said.

I stopped fiddling with the telephone wire.

'What do you mean, Harry? Carrying a firearm is against your law, let alone using it to threaten people. There is no doubt.'

'I'm not so sure, Aurelia. You must have been briefed on the current corruption stories.'

'That's local government building contracts, surely? And I thought trials in the north were fairly advanced?' I'd read in the papers this morning that the courtrooms were awash with sensation-seekers.

'Sadly, that's not the only area where brown envelopes of cash are being passed to public employees.'

'Wait a minute – are you saying your police are corrupt?'

'Absolutely not, but there are more cases closed without going to trial than there should be on purely statistical grounds.'

Gods! If you couldn't trust the law enforcers who could you trust? Our *vigiles* were dull and uninspired, but generally honest. It was a sought after job with good pay and attached privileges.

'But the new anti-corruption unit is making good progress,' he added.

'Well, I hope they're being severe when they uncover such traitors.'

'Not quite in the same way you Roma Novans are,' he shot back.

No, in Roma Nova that kind of betrayal would mean ten years in the grim prison out at Truscium.

'Look, Harry, Miklós and I are going to have to end our enquiry. I'm so sorry we can't do more. For some reason which he won't tell me, Plico has accelerated my recall. I fly home tomorrow.'

8

'No, we don't have a clue. That's why I needed you back here.' Plico sat on his side of the scruffiest desk in the foreign ministry. From the dust, assorted stains with and without a sheen of grease and ink marks, I was sure it hadn't seen a cleaner since the founding of Roma Nova at the end of the fourth century. The tone of his voice hovered somewhere between exasperated and desperate. 'At least you've got one complete brain cell, unlike the other halfwits taking up my office space.'

'Careful, Plico, that was almost a compliment.' I smiled at him.

'Humph.' He pushed a file marked *CELATA* towards me. Secret. Not unusual for the external affairs secretary (intelligence) to have in his office, but interesting that it was a blue one – international. 'It's one of these bloody jigsaw puzzles. It came up in "any other business" at the JELRC meeting and one of our bright sparks who normally sits in a corner counting file tags downstairs was there as a substitute and volunteered us to look into it. I've put him on making the tea for a few days as a reward.'

Poor young man, I thought. He was probably toiling over a load of paperwork in the archives now. The Joint European Liaison and Reporting Committee meetings weren't exactly the most exciting sessions, just worthy middle-rankers sent by their organisations to exchange nothing of significance in the most long-winded manner possible.

'So what's it doing on your desk if it's so unimportant, and why the urgent recall?'

'You know what I like about you, Mitela?' His eyes gleamed. 'You're not afraid to take a poke at me.'

'Well, you enjoy being insufferable and intimidating juniors. I know it's all a front.'

'Never mind that. We have three killings of second level leaders or serious influencers. One in Rome, one in Vienna and the third north in Batavia.'

'A police matter, surely?'

'Normally, yes. But too much of a coincidence within two weeks.'

'What's Roma Nova's interest?'

'Apart from young "Cassius Keen" offering to look into it, I don't like the feel of it. Too surgical and too widespread. I don't fancy having to explain to the imperatrix why we didn't act sooner when her chief councillor gets a bullet in her brain.'

'But the Praetorians would never let that happen!'

He gave me a cynical look.

'I know you're all superheroes in the Guard but this is a professional markswoman or man and it's all very carefully executed. Nobody can protect against an ambush. So we have to prevent that ambush happening. I want you to look through the file, talk to the boy who was at the meeting and tell me what you think. Tomorrow morning first thing will be fine.'

'Not a chance. I only flew in yesterday. Close of play tomorrow or nothing.' I stared at him, refusing to give way.

'Oh, very well.' He waved his hand. 'And welcome back to Roma Nova,' he said to the next file he dusted off from his in tray.

I hurried along the corridor to the general office and persuaded the chief clerk to allocate me a temporary office. I'd had to give up my old one when I'd been posted to London. The foreign ministry was desperately short of space, but they were at last building an annexe as witnessed by the not always muffled hammering from the builders and the infestation of displaced cupboards and cabinets stacked along the corridors.

The room boasted a small window, stacks of old files along one side and contained no furniture apart from two chairs and a desk.

After fifteen minutes reading the file and making some notes, I went back to the chief clerk.

'Where is Paulinus Axius, please? He's the one who represented us at the last JELRC meeting. I need to see him, stat. And please find me a telephone.' As he opened his mouth to protest, I said, 'I've already spotted the terminal box on the skirting board, so all you need to do is send along a techie with a screwdriver. Oh, and a handset. Today, if you please.' I turned and left.

Ten minutes later, somebody knocked faintly on my door which after a full second opened slowly. A short young man with a nervous expression and clutching half a dozen files edged into the room.

'Countess Mitela? I'm Axius,' he blurted out and stood still. He glanced at me, then at his files, then at the floor. He didn't look at all like Plico's "Cassius Keen", but like a rather diffident youngster.

'Come in and sit down, Paulinus Axius.' I smiled at him. 'Relax. I don't bite.' He slid into the chair on the other side of my desk and stared at me. 'Now show me what you've got and tell me about this JELRC liaison meeting.'

An hour later, we had a telephone, a cabinet and a large noticeboard on which we could pin connections and notes and a full complement of office paraphernalia. Axius was the most efficient supply officer I'd had in years.

'Can you log all these sightings and get photographs of the three victims and where the events took place?' I said. 'And mark connections, definite and tentative. Dig deeper into their biographies and itineraries. They're all prominent in their different ways. There must be something for us to find.' I glanced at my watch. 'I have to go to a Senate committee now, but I'll be back afterwards as long as it doesn't overrun. Leave what you've found on my desk if I haven't returned by six.'

The Senate building was an elegant marble construction with wide, gracious steps leading to impressive bronze doors, but inside the committee room the spirit was mean. The meeting dragged on as I suspected it would. Gods, we'd been discussing every *siliqua* and *follis* in a multi-million *solidi* intelligence and defence budget. I thought the *magistra militum* was going to self-destruct as she tried to answer the imbecilic questions put to her. As Roma Nova's chief soldier, she knew the difference between what she needed, what she wanted and what it would be nice to have. For most on the committee, their own national service was a decades-old memory. The only exception was Aemelius who'd served up to legate level before taking the purple stripe and entering the Senate. He'd rolled his eyes so many times, the committee president had asked if he was ill. I grinned at him when he replied tartly that he was only sick of all the narrow-mindedness and pussy-footing around. The silence was almost audible. A lot of coughing and fidgeting had followed, and the budget was passed at quarter to seven.

I hurried back across the forum to the foreign ministry. To my surprise, Axius was working away.

'What on earth are you still doing here?' I said.

'I couldn't leave it alone, *domina*. I think we have something. It's only a wisp of an idea and we need to check some things with other European security organisations.'

'Top marks for dedication. Now, show me.'

The next morning, at eight sharp, I made my way to Plico's office with Axius in my wake. Despite the chill outside, it was warm in the building, but I thought the shine on Axius's face was due to anxiety. Plico's assistant gave us her usual fierce look and waved us towards chairs at the side as she spoke into her intercom. I nodded but said nothing. Poor Axius looked as if he was going into the arena.

'Whatever you feel, don't let your nervousness show,' I whispered. I glanced at the assistant who had her back to Axius. 'She's a clerk, not a graduate researcher like you. And Tertullius Plico, who came up from an office boy, is, contrary to rumour, only a human being. Just answer any questions directly and honestly.'

Axius didn't look reassured.

Plico was standing by his security-glazed window looking out on the forum still lit by glowing streetlights. The office neon light highlighted the harsh lines of his face as he turned on hearing us approach his desk. He was frowning.

'Well?'

I waved to Axius to sit and took the other chair our side of the solid oak desk.

'First of all, I would like to bring Paulinus Axius to your attention, secretary,' I began. 'He has worked diligently and logically on the file into the small hours and correlated the scanty information into a paper for you.' I laid the two-page report on the curling blotter pad on Plico's desk.

'Noted. But have you discovered anything?'

'What we have is in the report, but essentially, it looks as if Axius's hunch is correct. Three killings of prominent, but second-tier, leaders cannot be coincidence. One or even two is possible, if unfortunate. Three, no. There is no ostensible connection, apart from their having had full access to their principals – all European political or business influencers. None of them went to the same university or advanced schools, they are not related in any way, nor sat on the same boards of commercial or charity organisations. Two were scheduled to attend the Paris economic forum, the third was about to go on secondment from his government to the EEA headquarters in Berlin.'

'Oh, brilliant! Is that it?' Plico looked at me, a flicker of disappointment in his eyes.

'The police reports vary between adequate and good, but the conclusion of all three is that each was a local tragedy. It was only pure chance they were mentioned at the JELRC meeting.' I smiled at Axius. 'Would you outline for the secretary how the subject came up, please?'

Axius swallowed, then drew himself up in the chair he was perched on.

'It was when they were settling the date of the next meeting, sir. The Italian Confederation officer, Bianchi, said he might not make it as there was a huge political furore over the killing of his minster's number two. He more or less joked that it had to look as if his department was doing something, even if he or the *carabinieri* didn't have any leads whatsoever.' Axius paused and took a breath. 'He seemed not completely unhappy that the deputy minister had been eliminated. Perhaps I'm reading too much into it, though.'

'No, the Italian spooks are a funny lot, especially the military ones. Always up to political shenanigans,' Plico said. 'Hopefully their new internal security organisation can keep its fingers in the right places.' He waved his hand at Axius. 'Carry on.'

'The New Austrian representative sympathised because she had a similar case – the number two at the central bank in Vienna. It had only come to the security service's attention because of a tenuous connection to the New Austrian royal family. When the Batavian representative exclaimed "What?" and outlined a similar killing, the room went quiet. She said the police had treated it as a political killing – somebody upset at a local issue.'

'So why did we end up with this on our plates?' Plico turned his full glare on Axius. A sheen of sweat broke out on the young man's forehead. I went to speak but Plico flicked his fingers at me.

'Sir, all I did was comment on the interconnectedness,' Axius continued. 'The chairman turned to me and asked me to develop my theory, which I did.'

'Oldest trick in the book,' Plico said, and rolled his eyes. 'Get the class swot to extend herself, then land all the shit on her, or him in your case. Mercury Esus! Didn't they teach you anything at the Central University?'

'I am not unaware of that stratagem, sir,' Axius said, looking straight back at Plico. I gave him top marks for that, and for the cooler tone in his voice. 'But they know, and we know, that Roma Nova has the best intelligence and operational services in Europe, if not the world. I did mention that we would expect full cooperation and er, financial contributions, *if* we considered taking it on.'

I bit my lips to stifle a chuckle.

'Ha! I'll give you this, boy,' Plico shot back. 'You have a hundred per cent brass neck.' Wisely, Axius didn't reply. 'I'd loved to have seen their faces when you asked them for money.' Plico smiled, although it was more a grimace. 'Did they agree?'

'They said they'd have to take it back to their ministers, etcetera, etcetera, but I think they were relieved, if I read them right.'

'Better send them all a heads of agreement, then. Oh, and don't forget to draw up the invoices.'

He nodded at Axius who took this as the signal to leave.

'What do you think?' Plico said once Axius had closed the door behind him.

'Axius shows great promise,' I said in my most demure voice.

'Oh, for Jupiter's sake, don't piss around the arena. You know what I mean.'

'Yes, but I'm savouring the moment when he stood up to you.'

'Am I that bad?'

'Yes.' I grinned at him. 'But back to the case. And I take it it's going live?'

'Gods, yes. The imperatrix is well protected, but we have to increase security on all senior ministers and the Senate president and warn prominent business people. Just a general recommendation – more of a reminder for the civilians. Don't want to start a panic. But some awkward type will inevitably start asking questions, so you'd better get cracking.'

9

Visiting Rome was always a pleasure, but it was a city that harked back too much to its ancient history and the labyrinthine bureaucracy that had plagued it, especially in the late empire. That same nostalgia had afflicted the Roma Novan envoy who had negotiated in the 1300s to purchase the site of our legation at the top of the Tarpeian Rock. But he'd had the sense to fortify the Hades out of it, given the bitter and lethal rivalry of the powerful families who'd ruled Rome in the late Middle Ages.

I still found it slightly ironic that the site, now designated as part of the Via San Teodoro, directly overlooked the ruins of the Forum Romanum and, from the top floor gallery, over the Palatine Hill.

Senior Centurion Bellania, the acting head of legation detail, met me at Rome's Transtiberina Airport. Tall, tough and polite, she explained that a meeting was arranged for the afternoon with an Italian representative of their new internal security service, the one whom Axius had met at the liaison meeting, and a major of the *carabinieri*. I'd been on a training exercise with the Italian army mountain troops special forces – a hard lot – but never encountered the *carabinieri*. And I'd gathered from Axius that Bianchi, the Italian spook he'd met at the JELRC, wasn't top-notch; depressing, to say the least.

'It's a first step, *domina*,' Bellania said, 'but one we'll have to go through if we're to get anywhere.'

'So, no meeting with the minister?'

'Apparently, his diary is full,' she said drily. '*Consultor* Galus will give you a full briefing.'

'Give me strength! Well, I'll take his and your advice, Bellania, but if I think they're obstructing us or even not cooperating, I'll bring in the heavy infantry, so to speak.'

She grinned, as any Praetorian would at that prospect.

At the legation, I dropped my bags in my guest room and over lunch with the legal *consultor* became even more depressed.

'I emphasised your status as former *nuncia* in the United Kingdom and as a senior diplomat representing Secretary Plico, and thus the imperatrix, to my contacts in the interior ministry, but they remain formal. I do wonder if there's something else going on.' He glanced at me between mouthfuls.

'Don't look to me, Galus,' I said. 'I only have the minutes of the liaison meeting and initialled heads of agreement. If you think there are other factors, tell me now.'

'There was some rumour of the late minister's deputy being in collusion over trafficking, but I must emphasise it's only a rumour. They fly round the Viminale like ravens in season. The prime minister's office is responsible for the internal security service since the corruption scandals a few years ago and their relations with the interior ministry at management level are positively glacial. The *carabinieri* despise them both.'

I put my knife and fork together and sat back.

'So we're going into a nexus of opposing forces, all of whom would rather fall on their swords than cooperate with us or each other. Perfect.'

The *carabinieri* building was set in a narrow street in an elegant part of Rome on the edge of a fenced square of lush trees and geometric paths. But the building itself looked like any other military barracks, although the ochre stucco exterior blended well with the other buildings.

A young woman in a navy uniform and impeccable make-up guided us into the functional office area. Walls were lined with a mix of black and white and coloured photographs from last and this century of unit members in various campaigns. Nostalgia from my own Praetorian service stirred as I glimpsed that mixture of determination, strength and contentment common to military personnel in the faces staring into the camera lens while challenging it.

The young *carabiniera* knocked on a door and ushered us in. A tall man in his forties rose from behind a metal desk and held out his hand.

'*Maggiore* Pirozzi. *Benvenuta, eccellenza.*'

'*Grazie molto,*' I said. 'I'm afraid that's more or less the limit of my Italian. Would you mind if we continued in English? Or French or perhaps Germanic?'

'But, of course, English is fine.' He smiled brilliant white teeth while I made a silent vow to brush up my language skills.

'First of all, thank you for this meeting, *maggiore*, and your cooperation. May I introduce *Consultor* Galus, head of the legal department here in our Rome legation, and Senior Centurion Bellania, Praetorian Guard, who is acting head of the legation security detail.'

Pirozzi nodded to Galus, then gave Bellania a measured look. He must have known about our diplomatic detail from basic intelligence reports, but perhaps seeing a female Praetorian in the flesh was a curiosity.

'And in turn, may I introduce Agent Matteo Bianchi from the state internal security service.' Pirozzi's smile faded as he turned to Bianchi, a brown-haired man with a waistline approaching middle age. The agent stood and shook hands, but withdrew his hand quickly. He glanced at my companions, but then brought his gaze back to me. I returned it stare for stare. After a few seconds he broke and sat down.

'To start,' Pirozzi said, 'we are of course very happy to work with the Joint European Liaison and Reporting Committee. We have prepared a file with our incident report, scene of crime report, photographs and biography of the victim. You will also find the report of the *medico legale*, who carried out the post-mortem examination.'

'That's very helpful, thank you. We'll read it carefully but just for now, *maggiore*, what was the cause of death?'

'Gunshot wound to the forehead from close range. The fatal round was from a Beretta 92.'

'So, the victim was facing the killer and knew he was going to die.' I turned to Bianchi and smiled insincerely at the security agent who shuffled in his seat. 'You were at the meeting the other day with my colleague Paulinus Axius, Agent Bianchi. What are your thoughts on the political aspects?'

'I have nothing to add to what I said at that meeting.'

'Really? Surely you must have made an analysis of the possible motives and potential fallout?'

'We can't see any motivation in the victim's background.'

'Perhaps he was involved in something suspicious in his off-duty or personal life? Did he have any criminal connections?'

Pirozzi fidgeted, but Bianchi shook his head, then studied his hands.

'Very well,' I said. 'Then the rumours of trafficking are false?'

Bianchi's head snapped up. 'Where did you hear that?'

'Are you denying it?'

'It doesn't come into our remit.'

'Oh, I would have thought bringing people across national borders illegally would have been.'

Bianchi said nothing but hit me with an incinerating look. I ignored it and turned back to Pirozzi.

'What leads are you currently following, *maggiore*?' I said.

'Unfortunately, there are none. We've carried out the usual analysis, questioned the official's work colleagues, family and friends – the usual investigations.'

'I see. I would like to visit the scene of the incident. Now, if we can arrange it.'

The blue light on the *carabinieri* car managed to clear a way through the traffic, but every other driver, especially those propelling smaller cars, pushed and swerved as if they were in a dodgem park. It was probably fortunate we couldn't hear the words spoken along with the undoubtedly rude hand gestures as the traffic hurtled round the streets. I glanced out of the back window. Bianchi was following us in his own vehicle, his face set and only one hand gripping the top of his steering wheel.

We stopped outside a four-storey building covered in dull salmon stucco in a street off the Piazza Navone. On the ground floor were a series of small shops and eateries like any ancient Roman *insula*. Police tape stretched diagonally across the door of a bar on the inside of which hung a sign stating '*Chiuso*'.

Pirozzi ripped the tape away, slipped a key in the lock and we entered. A long, thin room with a counter to the side and racks of coloured bottles behind gave way to a few tables, then booths towards the back. The sunlight from outside was reflected in the mirror behind the counter. Bellania fished two pairs of plastic gloves out of her bag and handed one pair to me.

'You permit?' I asked Pirozzi.

'Of course.'

Bellania switched the lights on. Glasses still on tables, fingerprint dust everywhere and blood spatter on the metal counter. I walked towards the rear of the room and left Bellania poking around the bar stools and the counter. Through a bamboo curtain I found a small storeroom, piled with crates of bottles, and a ceramic sink, and to the side, a half-glazed door leading to a miniscule courtyard. I turned the key and went out. Two metal barrels, a large overflowing refuse bin and a flowering shrub almost concealed another wooden door. The bolt was undone and I pulled it open. A tiny passage with what looked like a blank end. I walked along a couple of metres to the end and the passage turned ninety degrees. Now I could clearly see the Piazza Navone. I walked on into the bright sunshine of the square.

'Have you seen anything, *eccellenza*?' Pirozzi's voice behind me startled me for a second.

'Well, we can see how the assassin escaped. The killing took place around 7 p.m., so he could easily have slipped out the back and straight into the early evening passers-by and drinkers in the main piazza. Cleverly done.'

'You admire him?' Pirozzi frowned.

'No, but it helps to see a crime from the criminal's point of view. No, I—'

I caught my breath. Impossible. A blond-haired slim man, young, was staring at me. At only a few metres away, I couldn't miss the widow's peak.

'Tom,' I whispered and ran towards him. But he'd vanished into the crowd.

10

Major Pirozzi had my photo of Tom Carter copied and circulated that afternoon. I stressed he was a missing person, not a criminal, but would be grateful when they found him to call me immediately. I spent the rest of the afternoon studying Pirozzi's file with the aid of one of the younger Praetorians who was fluent in Italian. I could guess some of it – the words weren't far from Latin – but it would have been hubris to attempt to translate the finer points, the tenses and so on which were so important. But I was disappointed to find nothing out of the ordinary.

I called Pirozzi's office at seven to leave a message but was surprised to be put through to him.

'Are you working late, *maggiore*?'

'Just finishing, *eccellenza*. Nothing has come in yet about your missing friend. Perhaps something will emerge overnight.'

'I do appreciate it.' I glanced at my watch. 'If you're not rushing home, would you like to meet for a drink?'

There was a pause.

'Yes. Yes, that would be a very good idea.'

On Bellania's recommendation, I chose a quiet side street bar away from the tourist trail. She'd pressed one of the service communicators on me, an updated version of the prototype I'd used in Berlin a few years ago.

'I don't think I'll need backup, Bellania,' I said. 'I'm just going for a quick drink with a law officer from an allied state.'

'Secretary Plico would have a fit if he knew you were unescorted.' She looked at me sternly.

'Oh, for Mercury's sake! I'm not entirely past it.'

'Nevertheless.' She pushed the communicator into my hand.

Ten minutes after I left the legation, I was sitting at a table sipping a glass of Gavi behind the discretion of a smoked glass front window and waiting for Pirozzi. I remembered he was tall, but he seemed even taller as he strolled down the street towards me. Yet he covered the ground quickly. Dressed in a tailored leather jacket and tight, slightly flared grey trousers over a crisp white shirt, he had that indefinable elegant air of many Italian men. A sturdy gold chain around his neck caught the evening sun. Not a typical policeman. He went to the bar counter, ordered a drink and came to sit opposite me. When his beer arrived, he raised his glass to me then took a long swallow.

'Did you find anything interesting in the file I gave you?' he said as he set his glass down. I leant back in my chair.

'Nothing out of the ordinary. All very efficient.' I glanced round to check if anybody was within earshot, then leant forward cupping my chin in my hands.

'Now suppose you tell me what's really going on?'

He raised one eyebrow.

'Come on, Pirozzi. In your office you squirmed when I asked about criminal connections.'

'You surely can't expect me to be so unprofessional to answer such a vague question, *eccellenza*.'

'Aurelia, please. It's Emilio, isn't it?'

He nodded.

'If it isn't to have an off the record chat, why did you accept my invitation?'

'Why is Roma Nova pursuing this?'

'You should ask your colleague, Agent Bianchi.'

'He thinks it's a complete waste of time.'

'Really? I wonder why.' I looked up at him. 'Is he normally so sullen and uncooperative?'

'I've only worked with him once before but he bounced around on that case as if he had a firework up his—' He stopped and looked away as if embarrassed.

I laughed.

'If you want my honest opinion,' I said, 'I think Bianchi's on the take, or possibly under pressure. He was furious when I suggested the deputy minister had been involved in trafficking. Plus he wasn't too unhappy at the European liaison meeting my colleague attended a week ago when he mentioned the deputy's murder to the other representatives. Or perhaps he was just parading his ego to look tough.'

'Are you suggesting we mount a surveillance operation on a state security agent?'

'Yes. Unless you have any other ideas.'

He ran his finger down the tall beer glass, making a straight pattern through the drops of condensation. He glanced up.

'How long are you here for?'

'Only a few days. I have to visit colleagues north in Batavia and then Vienna.'

'Leave it with me.'

He left first and I finished my wine in peace. As I gathered up my jacket and scarf, my communicator buzzed. I hastened outside and found a brick wall to face. Glancing carefully left and right to check I had no observers, I lifted the set to my ear.

'Mitela.'

'Bellania. All well?'

'Affirmative,' I replied. I sighed. I suppose she was doing her job, but she seemed jumpy.

'Just a routine check,' came the terse reply.

'On my way back. Out.' I folded the lid back over and stuffed the communicator in my handbag.

I made my way down to the river to clear my mind. As I leant on the parapet and watched the lamplight reflected in the water I shivered, not with the cold but with the strange feeling that my many times ancestor must have looked out at the same bridge built in Cicero's time. We knew only a little about the original Mitelus before he travelled to Roma Nova. He'd been a soldier and a senator. His family had lived in a *domus*, a Roman town house, on the Palatine and owned a *latifundium*, a farming estate, somewhere out in Latium, but he'd never noted the location. I supposed then everybody knew where their friends and peers lived. And in the early years in Roma Nova, they hadn't had time or energy to sit at leisure writing their memoirs of their old life.

It started drizzling, so I looked around for a taxi. Gods, I must be getting soft. It was only about fifteen minutes' walk back to the legation. Rain never killed anybody, so slightly ashamed of myself, I set off along the shiny cobbles. Ten minutes later, just as the Vicus Jugarius narrowed and steps rose up left to the Tarpeian Rock, I shivered again, this time from the damp. Next time I wouldn't be so proud. A good brandy in front of a warm fire would be perfect when I got back.

A massive weight fell on me. Hands grabbed me. A stinging blow across my face. I kicked out as I fell and jabbed my fingers at eyes shining in a face centimetres from mine.

'*Porca puttana*,' a voice rasped and the hold on me relaxed. I rolled back and scrambled to my feet. Juno, my face stung. I crouched, hands and arms out, elbows bent ready. I snatched some quick breaths. Another figure from the left. I spun round and kicked him hard in the crotch. The first one, a big man, launched himself at me. I grabbed his collar and stuck my leg out. I heaved with all my remaining strength and he fell face first over my leg onto the hard cobbles. Breathing hard now, I spun round to finish the other one, but cold hard metal jabbed into the back of my neck.

I froze.

'Hands on head.' English, but not quite. 'You move, I shoot.'

The bigger thug was panting on the ground, the other groaning, holding himself between his legs. I shifted my weight on the balls of my feet. I could take the gunman.

'No, don't think of doing anything. I know you are good. But my finger is halfway squeezing trigger.'

Pluto in Tartarus.

'Kill her now, boss,' the big one said.

'Shut mouth,' he said in a low, but hard voice. He jabbed my neck. I grunted before I could stop myself. Sweat trickled down between my breasts. But there was something... something hovering I couldn't place. 'You, woman, no more poking nose in this that don't concern you. Leave Rome now. Go home.'

Then it clicked. But before I could form the next thought, pain exploded in my head with a bright flash of light, then darkness.

Gods, Vulcan himself was using my head as his anvil. Then the blessed relief of a cold cloth around my head. I opened my eyes slowly. I was in my room at the legation. Curtains drawn. A dim light in the far corner. I shifted my shoulders and pulled my elbows back to lever myself upward, but the world moved instead.

'Slowly, slowly now.' A woman's voice. A firm hand eased me back onto the pillows. 'Drink this,' she commanded, but in a soft voice. I sipped a faintly antiseptic-tasting liquid through a straw. When I'd finished, I let out a long breath. I put my hand to my aching face and found the skin greasy.

'It's to ease the bruising,' the gentle voice said.

'How did I get back here?'

'Senior Centurion Bellania found you,' the woman said. 'In fact, she's waiting to talk to you. Shall I let her in?'

I groaned, but inwardly.

Bellania wore an expression on her face like Mars on a bad day.

'I'm pleased to see you awake, *domina*,' she said in a dry voice.

'How long have I been out?'

'You were semi-conscious when we found you, on your knees, trying to stand up. The doctor has let you rest for a couple of hours. She will come and check you every few hours.'

'How did you find me?'

'Radio tracking on your communicator. Which was fortunate. Otherwise we might be visiting you in hospital as a pneumonia case.' She stared at me, her lips tight as if holding a flood back.

'I'm truly grateful, Bellania. Thank you.'

She waited for a full minute.

'Why didn't you call for a car, *domina*, or even take a taxi?'

'It was only fifteen minutes' walk and I wanted to clear my head.'

'Very well, but your personal security requirement has changed. You will be escorted everywhere from now on.'

'Really, Bellania, you exceed yourself.'

'I shall, of course, need to include this incident in my routine report, a copy of which will go to the secretary.'

Plico. This time I groaned aloud.

'You win, Bellania, but go away and let me rest.'

I woke next in the dark. The hands of the clock glowing green gave out the only light. Just after five. I switched on the bedside light, then lay back and wiped my face with my hand. Gods, what a mess. I sat up and drank water from a glass some kind soul had left for me. At least the thumping in my head had stopped; it merely ached. I had to get up and find out whose nest I had shaken enough to get a beating in the street. As I ran a bath to ease the aches in my body, I knew there was something I had to remember, but I didn't have a clue what it was.

11

There was something calm and businesslike about breakfast in the quiet of the dining room so early. Only the nightshift diplomatic staff eating before sleeping, a small group of Praetorians inputting coffee before starting the day, one or two office staff reading newspapers or their notes and stifling the odd yawn. None of the livelier chatting that would start in half an hour when the morning rush came in.

'*Domina*.' Bellania materialised at my side. She placed her coffee on my table and sat opposite me. 'You did not need to eat here. A steward would have brought you food in your room.'

'I'm fine, thank you. I can't lounge around in bed when there is work to do.' Before she could say anything else, I continued, 'I want to make a secure long-distance telephone call plus I need to book a video call to Secretary Plico this morning.'

'Of course. I will arrange it with the duty signals officer. The doctor is due to come and check you at 08.30 hours so after that.'

'I wouldn't expect anything else,' I retorted.

Plico's face was expressionless on the screen except for his eyes which searched my face.

'You're obviously getting somewhere, then, if the local lowlife has had a pop at you. Do you think it's anything to do with your meeting with Pirozzi earlier that evening?'

'I'm reluctant to think that Pirozzi was involved. It was only twenty minutes or so after I'd left the bar, so that would have been extraordinarily efficient.'

'True, he'd have to use official radio or find a phone box. Unless it was a set-up.'

'I'd rather put my money on that spook Bianchi, but I don't think it can be him either.'

'Oh? What great feat of intellectual thought brings you to that conclusion?'

Sometimes, I wanted to smash the screen when Plico went into his super-sarcastic mode, but I decided to ignore it.

'My attackers weren't trained personnel, they were more like thugs. But not opportunistic muggers. They knew who I was. The one in command spoke English, good pronunciation, but used funny expressions so he didn't sound native English. He told me to go home, so it was a warning, not a termination.'

'How generous of them.'

'No, it's not right.'

'Oh, you'd prefer to be dead?'

'Don't be facetious, Plico.' I flicked my fingers at him. 'I remember something clicked in my brain before I lost consciousness – a connection, but for the love of Mercury I can't remember what.' He wouldn't have seen me blush, but I felt deeply embarrassed as my memory was usually good.

'That's really helpful, isn't it?'

'Don't start!'

'Hm. We need to get on. I'll send young Axius to go and see the Batavians. You concentrate on getting to Vienna and see what the *Gendarmerie* have dug up. And have a word with your banker cousin while you're at it.'

The screen went blank.

Yes, Plico. No, Plico. Oh, I wouldn't have thought of seeing my cousin, Plico, when the murdered New Austrian had been a senior banker. I stopped fuming and called Pirozzi to report the attack. He was silent for a moment.

'I will send some officers out to see if we can find witnesses,' he said. 'I am truly sorry this has happened while you are visiting Rome, Aurelia. In the meantime, I will pursue that other line of enquiry we discussed.'

'I'm grateful. We've obviously shaken somebody, so let's see where that leads.'

Fortunately, Miklós was still at Thurswick Stud when I called.

'You just caught me,' he said. 'I've given Lambert my thoughts on the new bloodlines and I'm flying back to Roma Nova tomorrow.'

'Okay. I have to drop into Vienna on the way, then I'll be home. Give Marina a kiss and hug from me.'

'Of course, after mine.' He chuckled in that rich, sexy tone that sent shivers down my spine. 'Will you be long in Vienna?'

'A couple of days at most. Unless anything special happens.'

'Are you all right, Aurelia? You sound as if your shine has faded.'

I laughed back, admittedly forcing myself.

'And *you* sound so Hungarian when you say things like that.'

'Well, I'm no blunt speaking Roman. But you haven't answered my question.'

'I'm just a little tired, that's all. By the way, I'm seeing my cousin David for dinner tomorrow evening.'

'As I suspected, you're going on a little holiday before coming home.'

I knew he was teasing, but his lack of taking my job seriously sometimes really irritated me.

Next morning, Bellania escorted me through the VIP lounge at Rome's Transtiberina Airport.

'Thank you, senior centurion,' I said formally as I shook her hand. 'I hope your promotion comes through soon. You deserve it. Check with Major Pirozzi if you haven't heard within a couple of weeks and keep in touch. You have my number.'

'I will, *domina*. And Fortuna watch over your journey home.'

I glanced at her once more. I put more reliance in Air Roma Nova than the goddess, but I gave Bellania a nod then followed the hostess out onto the tarmac.

I was surprised to see Captain Licinia greet me at Wien-Maria-Theresia Airport. She didn't look any older than since I'd worked with her nearly six years ago on the Argentaria Prima and Caius Tellus investigation. She had perhaps gained a little roundness in her face. But why was she still heading up the legation security detail in Vienna? Surely her career would have progressed better with a home posting?

'Delighted to see a familiar face, Licinia,' I said, though, as I shook her hand.

'Welcome back, major,' she replied.

I smiled to myself. Licinia would never forget I had once been a Praetorian too. As we travelled along the motorway into the city to the legation in Marc-Aurel-Straße, she brought me up to date.

'We've been liaising with an *Oberleutnant* Hartl from the *Gendarmerie*.' She passed me a file and I skimmed through it. The victim was a Johannes Teiderstein, number two at the central bank in Vienna. As Axius had outlined in his report to Plico, the security service only picked it up because of a faint connection to the New Austrian royal family. His wife was a remote cousin. Gods, that was a complication we could all do without. Maria Amalia was a tough old biddy, not unlike our Imperatrix Justina.

'Hartl is efficient,' Licinia broke in. 'However, they seem to have no real leads. He says they're slogging through house-to-house enquiries, tracking movements, carrying out interviews with an ever-widening circle of colleagues and friends. The finance people will come in and check their accounts and returns once they can obtain a search order.'

'Where did the killing take place?'

'At Teiderstein's home, out in the Vienna Woods. It's an old family castle – hers – that he and his wife converted into an upmarket hotel. She runs it with her daughter and son. It was the wife that found him. He was sitting in the driving seat of his car in the stable block they use as a garage.'

'Poor woman. Have you been there?'

'Yes, but the problem is that it's in the middle of nowhere, surrounded by forest. I'll show you on the map when we get to the legation.'

Half an hour later, we poured over the survey map of the Wienerwald area, and specifically at the village of Beblburg bei Wien. Sure enough, about a kilometre to the north-east of the settlement was Schloss Bebl.

'They came through the woods, then,' I said, standing up and stretching my back. 'Easy enough in a four-wheel drive or a motorbike along those tracks, then on foot.' I smiled at Licinia. 'Well, that's how I'd do it, then over the wall and into the stables. Probably used a silencer. Nobody to see or hear. Damn.'

'Hartl mentioned there was a big dance on at the castle during the evening, so the noise may have covered the sound of the gunfire,' Licinia added. She took a step back from the table. 'Walther P38 pistol. The 9mm round went straight through and ended up in the leather of the back seat, so the victim was shot *in situ*, point blank, Hartl concludes.' Licinia looked at me. 'This isn't really my area of expertise, but this looks like a managed execution.'

'So it would seem.' I glanced at her. 'Well, you'd better introduce me to this Hartl.' She looked down and for half a second, I thought I saw her blush.

Licinia went to her office to call the *Gendarmerie* and arrange the meeting while I studied the reports. The same deliberate approach marked both attacks. Both men were in familiar surroundings where they would have felt safe and relaxed. But what was Teiderstein doing in his car in the garage when there was a big event on in the hotel?

Oberleutnant Hartl shook my hand and smiled before gesturing Licinia and me to chairs on the other side of his desk. He was medium height, dark haired with brown eyes; he could have been a Roma Novan from his appearance.

'Unfortunately, we are not making much headway, *Frau Gräfin*, although we're continuing our investigation in the traditional manner. Everybody in the area knew *Herr* Teiderstein and his wife, Barbara. Quite a lot of the locals work at Schloss Bebl. We're running background checks on them, of course, plus on the casual staff hired for the evening of the big dance. The hotel uses an agency in Vienna and it seems there's a pool of regulars who help out on these occasions.' He handed me an envelope. 'We've prepared some background information on the victim for you, but it's fairly vanilla, you might say. The only odd thing was the smell of marijuana.'

'So he'd slipped out to the garage for a quick smoke? To relax?'

'Perhaps,' Hartl replied in a neutral tone.

'I'm sure you've done the usual enquiries about grudges and quarrels,' I continued. 'And checked there was no trouble between husband and wife? No lovers or mistresses on either side?'

'All covered,' he said and smiled. 'Nothing.' His face became serious. 'We reported the death as a priority to the security service because of the strategic nature of Teiderstein's job and his wife's connections, but they don't have anything on either of them.'

'Too perfect?'

'The odd parking fine, and she's filed her tax late a few times. The daughter was done for possession when a student but that's it. Nothing else that we can see. The financial experts are ready to start checking both husband's and wife's financial backgrounds and statuses, but it takes a while to persuade a judge to give a written order when it comes to the banking world. If there's anything political, I'm hoping it may emerge from *your* investigation.'

'We know he was going to the same conference as the Batavian victim, but there is no other connection and none to the Italian,' I said. 'Should I speak to your colleague in the security service – the one who was at the European liaison meeting?'

'Her report is in your papers.' He pointed to the envelope. 'I don't know if speaking to her will help, but I'll certainly arrange a meeting if you think it will.'

'Very well. I'll read through this first and come back to you if I have any questions.' I stood, shook his hand and walked to the door. Licinia, however, was whispering something to Hartl. Thanking him for the meeting? But her face was serious, and she frowned at him. He shrugged, then nodded his head.

We walked in silence to the front door of the *Landeskriminalamt* station.

'Problem with Hartl?' I asked as she pulled the door open for me.

'Not at all, major. Just a local practical point.'

'Nothing that's going to affect the investigation?'

'Absolutely not.'

I had to be content with that, but I sensed there was more.

That evening, the legation car dropped me off at a modern angular building of glass and polished steel set in the middle of the Vienna

Stadtpark. You wouldn't have thought it was one of Vienna's most exclusive restaurants. The soft lights reflected the layered leaves of decades-old stately trees which didn't seem to mind the brash incomer in their midst. I walked up the broad steps and was greeted by a smiling man in a perfect suit moulded to his figure.

'David Soane, please. I'm his guest.'

He bowed and ushered me over to a window seat where a medium-height man with brown wavy hair and pale eyes sat. He smiled then stood and kissed my cheek.

'Aurelia, it *is* lovely to see you.' He signalled to the waiter who immediately lifted a bottle from the ice bucket and poured a glass of champagne for me.

'I hope you don't mind, but I've ordered for us already.' He said that with such a warm voice full of Viennese charm that although I would normally insist on making my own choices, I didn't have the heart to protest. Although British, David headed Soane's Vienna, a branch of a private British bank established for over two hundred years.

We shared a great-grandfather; Matthew Soane, English, from London. Following tradition, he'd joined the family firm. He'd frowned on his eldest son, Henry, my grandfather, when he'd emigrated to Roma Nova to marry my grandmother. Peter John, my grandfather's younger brother, had taken over the business in London, expanding it through Europe as Britain became an industrial powerhouse. Vienna, then the centre of European banking, had hosted their first overseas branch. Despite their father's disapproval, Peter John and Henry had remained good friends and Soane's Vienna handled several Mitela overseas investment portfolios.

I'd always liked David; he'd helped me before when I'd been tracking rogue silver trading across Europe a few years ago. Now I was treading into his banking environment, a very closed community in Vienna.

'David...' I fiddled with the smaller fork on the immaculate damask cloth. Gods, my mother would have been appalled. I drew my hand back.

'Aurelia?' my cousin replied, with a beguilingly open expression on his face.

'You've probably guessed why I'm in Vienna.'

'Yes, I wondered when one of Plico's ferrets would turn up. Not that I class you as such, of course. More like a polite but tenacious lynx.'

I didn't know whether to be flattered or furious. An exquisite confection of pike, lemon and herbs arriving on the table in front of me stopped my first retort. I took a mouthful and my irritation melted in the delicate and sensual taste that conquered my taste buds.

'David,' I said after a pause. 'That was harsh, but I understand how upset you and your colleagues are. But I've been mandated by JELRC, sorry, the Joint European Liaison and Reporting Committee—'

'Yes, I do know who they are.' He looked at me like a patient professor with a dull pupil. But then the bankers had an extremely good commercial intelligence network of their own, so of course he knew.

'We think the shooting here in Vienna is linked to two others – one in Rome and one in Batavia. A colleague is in the Hague at present. I'm here to talk to you.'

'Well, that's direct enough.' He leant forward. 'Teiderstein's death is a shock, of course. He was a solid, if not particularly innovate central banker. The jockeying to replace him has already started.'

'Are you in the running?'

'Good heavens, no! And besides, I'm not a New Austrian national.'

'Ah, then you're free to give me your assessment. Was he up to anything?'

He glanced at me, then away. So there was something.

'Rumours are always pernicious. My policy is to disregard them unless proven otherwise.' He sipped his wine, the glass full of light from the reflection of the table candle.

'But?' I persisted.

'Surprisingly for a person instrumental in running a national economy, his own family one seems, er, ramshackle. His wife's tax returns, for instance, are always questioned, so questionable.'

'Perhaps she needs to sack her accountant.'

'She's married to him. Or was.'

'Ah.'

'And the castle has a large loan secured against it. The rumours I mentioned suggest there may have been the odd default in repayments.'

'So he's in money trouble. Who's the lender?'
'Really Aurelia, that's confidential.'
'It's not you, is it?'
'Good Lord, no!'
'Then you can tell me.'
'You are so persistent.'

I said nothing. I smiled, attempting to be sphinx-like. He shrugged.

'I've known – knew – Johannes Teiderstein for many years,' he said. 'My judgement was that he was a solid risk.' He fidgeted in his chair and glanced around the restaurant before looking at me again. 'But I learnt something recently through a backchannel…… and this is entirely unattributable, you understand,' he added. I nodded, barely breathing. Here it came. 'His loan was provided by a Helvetian Confederation financial company – Gebrüder Wyss Finanz.'

Gods, what a cliché, but I kept my face passive.

'But their corporate structure is strange,' David continued. 'You know how strong the EEA money laundering regulations are, but somehow – call it gut instinct – I don't think Wyss's sources of funds are entirely above board.'

'Go on.'

'They have three tiers of holding or management companies, but the turnover doesn't justify it. And their operations, while significant, are fewer than you would expect for a financing company of that type.' He glanced at me. 'There's nothing obviously wrong, but it's a strange choice of lender for a man like Teiderstein. It's none of my business, but professionally, I'm deeply curious about the terms of this loan.'

So was I. I had to call Hartl as soon as I was back at the legation.

'I haven't spoken to Barbara, the wife, yet except by telephone to offer my support,' David continued. 'It doesn't seem dignified to harry her at the moment.'

'What's she like? As a person, I mean.'

'Gracious, pleasant, hard-working, a little superior on occasion because of her family connections.'

I groaned inwardly; we had the type in Roma Nova among the Twelve Families.

'Why don't you come and meet her when I pay my formal visit? As my cousin, there could be no objection,' he added.

'I don't think I'd better. I'm part of the investigation team.'
He paused and looked at me steadily.
'Sometimes, you take your sense of duty too seriously, Aurelia.'

12

Hartl and I drove out to the Vienna Woods the next morning followed by two white liveried police cars. He suppressed a yawn. Being woken at midnight, then having to get up for 8 a.m. at the court to lobby the judge to issue the warrant then and there must have cost him several hours of sleep. Apparently, the information from David had been enough for the judge. I'd stressed it was only a rumour, but had to agree with Hartl that a rumour from super-cautious and much respected David Soane probably equated to state's evidence from any other individual. But I was still recovering from my surprise that it was Licinia who had answered Hartl's house phone in the middle of last night.

Hotel Schloss Bebl was a plain four-storey building with pepperpot towers at three of the corners. The slate-covered coned roofs shone in the morning sunlight as we approached the hill the old building perched on. Window boxes full of red and purple flowers prevented it from looking like something out of a grim fairy tale. But in contrast to the medieval-fortress look at the front, at the back on the more gradual slope of the driveway, a classic nineteenth-century addition decorated with a variety of national flags over a shallow porch seemed more welcoming. We parked in the gravel-covered courtyard.

A doorman dressed in maroon coat, cap and smile pulled the glazed door open and we stepped into a grand hall of marble, gold and hunting green. An elegant blonde woman rose from a leather armchair. A royal blue wool dress stretched over her slim figure and her make-up was impeccable. She could have walked out of a fashion magazine. Even her elegant movement came from the catwalk.

'*Frau* Teiderstein? My name is *Oberleutnant* Hartl from the Vienna *Gendarmerie*.'

She shook his hand very quickly and let it drop.

'And this is?' she said in a cool, assured tone and looked me up and down.

'May I present *Frau Gräfin* Mitela, a liaison officer.'

'Mitela?' She gave me a smile. 'One of the Roma Nova families?'

I nodded.

'Please, sit. And you too, *Herr Oberleutnant*,' she added. 'How can I help you?'

'I need to ask you some further questions about your late husband's affairs.'

'Oh, really! Is it really necessary? I've given you my statement and so have my staff. What else is there?'

'We need to look at your husband's financial transactions including any loans and share dealing. In fact, we need full access to his and your files, especially any international dealings.'

'No,' she said almost too quickly. She rubbed her thumb and first finger together, uncrossed then recrossed her legs.

Hartl drew out an envelope from his inside jacket pocket and handed it to her.

'Here is the legal order. We will be as careful as possible, but you must understand we need to be thorough. Would you please give me the keys to his desk and any filing cabinets? And to yours.'

'I'm phoning my lawyer.' She sprang to her feet, her face flushed. 'You will be lucky to still have a job after this,' she spat out as she strode off.

'Nice,' I said.

He didn't reply but spoke into his radio. Three uniformed officers and a plainclotheswoman arrived, took instructions from Hartl and went off in different directions.

'Oh, well, let's start in his office.' Hartl's voice drooped; in light of Barbara Teiderstein's uncooperative attitude, he sounded resigned to hours of difficult searching and sifting. From his book-lined study, Teiderstein had a magnificent view over the valley; trees, a pretty church, mountains reflecting the sun in an azure sky. What on earth would distract a man who had a senior, well-paid job with direct access into government circles, a more than comfortable home, a family business which attracted a five-star clientele and an attractive, well-connected life partner?

A crack broke into my thoughts. Hartl had jemmied the desk drawer, then lifted it and emptied the contents onto the gold-blocked leather inlaid top.

'I'll go through this lot if you want to open up the bureau,' I said. 'There must be a private safe somewhere as well.' I flicked through the cards and papers from the drawer.

'I've told Maurer to try to persuade the receptionist to open the hotel one,' Hartl said.

'Maurer?'

'The sergeant who was driving the first patrol car behind us. He's got a good chat-up technique, man or woman.' Hartl flashed a quick grin at me. 'But you're right,' he continued more soberly. 'Damn that woman. I suppose I'll have to arrest her for obstruction. That'll look good.'

'There's nothing here,' I said after a few momentes, pointing to the drawer contents. 'Shall I go and have a word with her?'

He shrugged. 'If you think you can get through.'

I found Barbara Teiderstein in her office behind the reception desk. She quickly removed a pair of glasses and looked up with her best professional hospitality smile.

'I realise it must be disturbing for you, *Frau* Teiderstein, as you have so much to occupy you in running your hotel, but we do need to pursue all leads to investigate your husband's murder.'

'There is no need for the police to pry into our personal affairs.' Her voice was subdued. She must have received no rescue from her lawyer.

'Ah, but there is. *Herr* Teiderstein was mixed up in some, let's call it anomalous, cross-border financial affairs. Given his position at the central bank, we must uncover the exact nature of these to see if there was a motivation from that direction.'

She frowned.

'I'm sure you wouldn't be mixed up in these affairs. You must be equally interested in finding the truth, I would think. And preferably before any of the press get wind of it.'

'Is that a threat?'

'Certainly not.,' I said. 'Merely an observation. But they do love a juicy scandal linked to what they perceive to be the privileged classes.' I gave her my most sympathetic smile.

She folded her papers and laid them in an elegant walnut tray on her desk. In a flash of bright red nail polish, she stretched out her fingers, opened a drawer and took out a bunch of keys and a slip of paper. I glimpsed a row of handwritten figures.

'Come with me,' she snapped.

'Gratuliere,' Hartl said as we drove back to Vienna proper along the new *autobahn*. 'I thought we'd have to bring in the whole wrecking team.'

'Wrecking team?'

'Technical search unit, but they love to glamorise themselves, so they pinched that name from an American movie.'

I chuckled. 'Our *vigiles* have a similar sense of humour.'

'We'll analyse all this lot in detail.' I glanced at the back seat covered with archive boxes of paper and data tapes. 'I'll let you know if or when anything significant comes up,' he continued. 'Of course, we'll send through a full report as soon as we've completed the analysis.'

'Thank you. One thing that bothers me is that both the Rome shooting and the murder here suggest the victim faced the killer. Both have GSR from a commonly used local weapon.'

'Have you heard from your colleague in Batavia?'

'No, but I have a feeling I'm not going to be surprised by what he'll report.'

Back at the legation, I called home, but the steward said Miklós wasn't there. Neither was he at the farm out at Castra Lucilla. Odd. So odd that I thought of checking to see if he'd passed through Roma Nova border control. No, that would be overreacting. I twisted the braided telephone cable between my fingers. I was being silly. He might have stopped off somewhere or gone to see one of his trading 'friends'. But when I'd called him yesterday, he'd been so definite about going straight home this morning on the early flight from London.

I ordered a sandwich from the dining room while I sat down to go through Hartl's notes again. As soon as I finished, I'd call Axius in Batavia to see if he was making any headway. If his victim had been dispatched in the same way...

A sharp knock on the door interrupted my thoughts. Licinia held a small white envelope in her hand.

'Excuse me, major, but this note was handed in for you while you were out.'

'Come in for a moment and shut the door,' I replied. I waved her to the chair in front of my desk. 'It's none of my business so feel free not to answer, but do I get the impression you and *Oberleutnant* Hartl are closer than is usual between a member of the legation protection detail and the local scarabs?'

She bridled for an instant, but the expression on her face quickly returned to passive.

'Yes, it is none of your business, but yes, we are partners. The *nuncia* is aware. Obviously.' Her voice was defiant, almost insolent.

'I think it might have been courteous to have given me a hint as Hartl is the *Gendarmerie* investigating officer.'

'It doesn't affect my duties, nor this investigation.'

'No, but it might have led to embarrassment somewhere along the line.'

She stiffened but said nothing. The only noise was a clock beeping as it reached the hour.

'I apologise for my oversight, *domina*.'

Now I knew I was in her bad books when she didn't call me major.

'I didn't mean to pry, Licinia, and I wish you every continuing personal happiness, but it would have been helpful to know.' She relaxed a few millimetres. 'Now what's the message you have for me?'

I flicked it open and scanned it. My heart thumped as I read it again.

'No. They can't,' I croaked. My hand trembled and I fell back against my chair.

Licinia leapt up and came round to my side of the desk.

'Major? What is it?'

Unthinking, I held out the note – a crudely pasted series of letters cut from newspapers.

> YOU WERE WARNED IN ROME.
> STOP POKING YOUR NOSE IN
> OR WE WILL TERMINATE FARKAS.

13

Not a prayer!' Plico's face in the black and white image was set hard as concrete. 'We don't know if they've got him or if it's pure bluff.' He paused. 'Probably the second.'

'How in Hades can you be so bloody sure?' I wanted to smash the screen in front of me. The low murmur of human voices in the Vienna legation comms room that ran above the machine noise stopped. I was in one of the booths and wearing headphones, but the door was open behind me and I'd probably shouted at full volume. I swallowed hard, turned and mouthed 'sorry' to Licinia hovering behind me. She half turned, snapped her fingers at operators in the open room. The murmuring and sound of tapping on teleprinters resumed.

'Look, I'll check with London to see if they can confirm he got on the plane and ditto here with the border police to see if and when he arrived at Portus Airport,' Plico replied. And we'll get the *vigiles* to check your farm. Your steward's sure Farkas hasn't slipped upstairs and is sleeping off a hangover?'

'Juno, you are such a bastard sometimes, Plico.'

'Yes, I know.' But he didn't grin as he normally would when being quasi-insulting.

'I'm getting on the next flight home,' I said. 'Nothing political has come up with Teiderstein yet. The police here are plodding on and they've promised to let us know straight away if anything significant emerges. Licinia is liaising. She's pretty damn sharp.'

'Now you're sounding reasonable, Mitela. Alarms are going off in my head.'

'I'm going to pack. I'll be on the seven o'clock flight.'

I handed my voucher and diplomatic passport over to the check-in clerk at regional desk at Wien-Maria-Theresia Airport only forty minutes before the flight. She insisted on trying her Latin out on me; terrible accent, but she was sincere so I smiled encouragingly. My suitcase disappeared into the maw of baggage handling and I clipped my handbag shut. The gate was being called so I set off quickly. But a purple-suited figure holding a small radio intercepted me. It was the driver who'd brought me to the airport.

'Captain Licinia's compliments, ma'am, but she must speak to you.' The driver thrust the radio set at me and stepped back.

'Mitela,' I said into the microphone.

'Licinia. Flash message from Plico. Divert to Paris.'

'Repeat that,' I snapped.

'Your target is in Paris area, repeat Paris.'

I glanced at the driver. She gave back no reaction. My heart started thumping.

'Understood.'

'Full briefing with driver meeting you at Paris-Leclerc Airport. Next flight forty minutes. Reservation made,' Licinia's disembodied voice rapped out. *'Bon voyage,'* she added.

By some miracle, they managed to retrieve my suitcase just before it was loaded on the Air Roma Nova flight home. The navy blue case with oversized zips seemed so mundane. I pulled it into the ladies' and changed into slacks and a warm jumper, then plaited my hair and pinned it up. I was shedding my diplomatic persona, my mind whirring as if I were going into action.

At Paris-Leclerc, just after nine, the legation driver who met me handed me a puzzled look and an envelope. He said little as he wove through the evening traffic on the way into the city centre. I studied the envelope contents, but the 'full briefing' turned out to be a single sheet timed an hour ago with few details. Miklós had checked in on the London to Roma Nova flight, but didn't go through immigration at Portus Airport.

Sighting at West London Airport at Air France gate at time of Paris flight shortly after his scheduled one to RN. More to follow as facts emerge. T. Plico.

The gods let me be not far behind. But why in Tartarus had Miklós come to Paris? Maybe Plico would have found out more by the time I reached the Paris legation. Had the killers really got Miklós, or were they bluffing? I daren't risk it. I had to assume the worst.

Every minute I was delayed, Miklós was in danger. The rain wasn't helping but Juno, the driver was taking forever. I leant forward to tap him on the shoulder to tell him to put his foot on it, but drew back. He was doing his best in the traffic and he knew where we were going. He would know the shortcuts.

Calm down, Aurelia!

I could do nothing until we arrived but I couldn't stop fidgeting. I tried to divert myself by remembering what I knew about the legation here. Not much. The original one had been destroyed by the Paris uprisings in the 1790s but we'd re-established it half a century later on the north bank in a gracious building set in gardens to rival even the British Embassy.

At last! The car swung into the entrance, the security gate slid shut behind us. Lining the drive to the front door of the building, spaced globe lights hung on delicate swan neck posts and shed soft, almost fairy light. Inside, in the vestibule, a tall man in Praetorian barrack uniform of beige and black rose to greet me. His expression was solemn.

'Good evening, *domina*. Lieutenant Celcus, head of the legation detail. Please come with me.'

He led the way through a door behind the public reception desk, then along a blue-carpeted corridor. At the end, he entered a keycode on the pad by the door and ushered me in. It was the comms room; bright lights, the smell of machine oil and barely circulated stale air. Another one. Celcus strode over to the duty signals officer's desk and held out his hand. She gave him a folded piece of teleprinter paper and a fax sheet and glanced down quickly, then back at him. He said nothing but just handed them to me.

The long thin face topped with black curls that I had only kissed a few days ago stared out of the grainy fax sheet. His face was unshaven and harsh lines distorted the skin round his nose and mouth. But it was Miklós. He was holding up today's newspaper. I read the message. Twice.

BACK OFF, GO HOME AND HE LIVES.
WE KNOW WHERE YOU ARE.
NO HEROICS OR HE DIES.

I touched the base of my throat and swallowed hard. After a few moments I unfroze.

'What time did... did this come through?' I stuttered.

'The fax went to the foreign ministry at home while you were in the air. You can see from the date stamp, the message followed it a few minutes later and was then forwarded here shortly before you arrived,' Celcus said in a measured tone.

Hades, I should have seen that for myself without his prompt. He must have thought I was an idiot. I looked at my watch. Ten thirty. They must have taken Miklós nearly twelve hours ago.

Gods, a second death threat within hours of the first. But if they really knew where I was, they would have sent it to the legation here.

'Very well,' I said, pushing down my panic. 'Tell me what steps you've taken so far.'

'We've alerted the Paris police about the kidnapping; they'll liaise with their organised crime service. I've also arranged for a contact from the French internal security service to come and talk to you.'

'What time?' It would be in the morning now. Another six hours' delay at least.

'He's here now.'

I looked at Celcus. A fast worker.

In a small, plain office along the corridor, a short dark-haired man with a receding hairline and wearing jeans and a leather bomber jacket rose from a chair and held his hand out in greeting.

'Régis Morin, foreign liaison, at your service. We have circulated details of your national, *madame,* and alerted our field agents to look out for him.'

'Actually, he's Hungarian but resident in Roma Nova,' I said almost mechanically. 'Our protection covers him.'

Morin spread both hands in a quick gesture. 'Regrettably, we have little spare capacity to search actively – budget cuts, you know – but we will give full support and access to our intelligence to Lieutenant Celcus and his colleagues. But I can at least confirm your subject came through Paris-Leclerc towards midday. After that, we have nothing.'

He looked at me as if with infinite regret. Pluto, it would be like looking for a grain of spelt in a municipal granary. But I couldn't sit here on my hands. I was hardly aware of Morin leaving, but when Celcus shut the door behind him, I flopped into the chair the Frenchman had just vacated. I rubbed my forehead and tried to think.

'Very well, Celcus, you know the ground here. Do you have any kind of plan?'

'He could be anywhere, *domina*. Not necessarily in the city or even the suburbs. They could have moved him across the border into one of the Germanic states or even Spain.'

I clenched my hands together in my lap.

'But using intelligence from Morin's people, I have sent out three two-person patrols to check locations known to be used by some of the gangs. But as you know, if these places are known to the authorities, the kidnappers are unlikely to use them again. Two more will relieve them at five.'

He was so calm and reasonable I wanted to scream at him. But he was right.

'Secretary Plico has scheduled a video call to you at seven thirty tomorrow morning to assess intelligence to date and decide strategy.'

'I'll go out with your early morning patrol before that,' I said.

'I'm sorry, *domina*, but Tertullius Plico said that under no circumstances were you to leave the legation until he had spoken to you.'

14

At six the next morning, I attacked the fitness machines in the basement gym, then went for a sprint several times round the legation garden. The early chill combatted some of the hot frustration at Plico, my sense of helplessness, and the knowledge Plico was right. I *had* been exhausted. The patrols Celcus had sent out knew the area and would have been far more effective than I could have come anywhere near to.

I showered then headed down to the dining room for breakfast. Legations were deemed to be like a *familia* at home, so everybody ate together. But there was no sign of Celcus. After demolishing a plateful of eggs, spelt bread, cheese and olives, I poured myself a second cup of coffee and was contemplating the basket of fresh pastries, warm and oozing with butter, when a beige and black figure walked up to my table.

'The lieutenant's compliments, *domina*, and would you like to come to his office at your convenience?' she said in a voice trying not to allow excitement to creep into it. She failed.

'Tell me,' I commanded.

'I think Lieutenant Celcus should give you the news.'

Coffee and croissant abandoned, I rushed out and upstairs.

'It's not a hundred per cent certain,' Celcus said, 'but one of Morin's local officers has reported something. He lives in a village in the Loire Valley area and although he keeps claiming to be a lowly civil servant, everybody knows he's a spook. The local garage owner who lives next door to his business told him some foreigners had fuelled up late last night just as the garage owner was closing around 8 p.m.'

'What kind of "foreigners"?' I asked, hardly able to breathe.

'English, but one of them in the back was dozy and spoke gibberish. The garage owner was curious and thought the man might be drunk or ill and offered them water. But they refused.'

'Gibberish?'

'Nothing he'd heard before, but when Morin told his contact to find a Hungarian station on the wireless and play it to the garage owner, the old boy shrugged and thought it could be the same.'

'Description?'

'Dark, like a southerner, curly hair.'

I clasped the palm of my hand to my mouth. It had to be Miklós.

'Right, quickest way to get there?' I snapped.

'Morin has pursuit vehicles ready and waiting,' Celcus began.

'Sir!' The young comms clerk who had interrupted my breakfast burst into the room. 'Secretary Plico is on the video link. He says I must fetch Countess Mitela to the screen, stat.'

Hades. Plico was never *not* in urgent mode.

'Well?' I said to the screen as I pulled on the headphones in the comms room booth.

'I see you've woken up snotty as usual,' he groused at me.

'What's so urgent? We have a live lead here and cars waiting to pursue it. Every minute is vital.'

'Of course it is, but you needed your rest last night. You'd have been bugger all use this morning otherwise.'

'Conceded. Now we have to get going, so—'

'If I can get a word in edgeways,' Plico interrupted 'you may like to know that I've called in a favour and got you a ride. Tell your go-faster driver to go to the *Armée de l'Air* base east of Versailles. There's a spec ops unit there who'll give you a lift to just outside Saumur in under the hour.' I stared unbelieving at the harsh face in the screen. He flicked his fingers at me. 'Well, get going then, or are you stuck to the chair?'

• • •

Six of us, all in civvies, sprinted under the flailing blades towards the door of the troop carrier helo. As we clambered on board, the pilot bent his arm and rotated his forearm at us – ready for immediate take-off. The helo roared off the ground as if sucked by force into the sky. I gasped as the clip on my helmet strap dug into my flesh. But the harsh thumping of the main rotor reflected my heart doing the same. It had to be Miklós. Gods, when I got hold of the bastards who'd kidnapped him, they were going to regret it for the rest of their lives. Their target was me. How dared they go for the soft option of my family? Surely they knew retribution by any Roma Novan would be severe?

Fingers on my arm; Celcus handed me two magazines of fifteen rounds and a compact pistol, a 9mm. I checked it, made it safe and eased it into the tiny holster attached to my belt. The French spec ops sergeant who briefed us added that they were evaluation weapons and please to return them. Morin said a word that made the sergeant bark out a chuckle and glance at me but he didn't tell us the meaning. That sergeant was now sitting on one of the fold-down seats the other side of Celcus.

I spent the hour poring over the map and familiarising myself with the area. It looked like a charming village from the photos Morin had given us, but beautiful stones sometimes hid grim tragedy.

We touched down at the civilian aero club, tumbled out and scuttled like crabs away from the drop zone as the helo rushed back up to the sky. Morin went forward to one of the cars and shook hands with the driver who turned out to be the local agent, Duvalier. A tall man with brown hair which flopped over his face, he drew out a leather-bound notebook and flipped a page over.

'I had another word with the garage owner – bit of a surly sod – but he said he noticed the car not only because of the 75 number plate for Paris but because it was a foreign make, a Swedish one. Not exactly common in rural France.' His eyes gleamed. 'We've found it. It's big and was parked with its front end poking out of the garage next to a run-down farmhouse on the eastern edge of the village.'

'Access?' I said.

Duvalier flipped over another sheet and pointed to places on a sketch map.

'One road running south along the property perimeter where there's a pond,' he said. 'Another to the west, then a farm track along the other side. Best of all, there are trees to the north-west and south-east of the farmhouse.'

'Perfect,' I replied. 'How far is the village from here?'

'Ten minutes south-west of here.' He glanced at his watch.' We can get there before the road gets busy with the lunchtime rush.'

'Very well,' I said. 'First, synch radios.' Celcus handed out small transceivers and demonstrated how to use them. The Frenchmen turned them over and over, their professional air dissipated by sheer curiosity. 'There are six of us,' I continued. 'We'll drop off in three pairs of two, one pair at the edge of each of the woods near the house. Celcus and I will take the farm track leading directly to the farmhouse. That way we'll encircle the place. Be ready to move on my mark. One click on the radio – prepare to move; two clicks – immediate advance to contact.'

'One moment, *madame*,' the French sergeant said. 'Surely you will wait here. This is a task for men.'

Morin muttered *'Imbécile'*. Celcus stepped forward so that he nearly trod on the French soldier's toes.

'*Major* Mitela was leading special forces operations while you were still in school, sergeant,' he almost hissed. I laid my hand on Celcus's forearm.

'Stand down, lieutenant. It's just a matter of ignorance. Perhaps unlike Agent Morin, the sergeant has never worked with us before. He will learn.'

Celcus and I had the good fortune to be sheltered by hedgerows along most of the track to the farmhouse. In the few gaps, we just crouched down, then continued. After fifty metres, the hedge petered out to be replaced by a metre-high crumbling drystone wall. Ten metres further on we came to the farm buildings.

In front of us lay a part-cobbled, part-concrete farmyard. To our left sat a barn, doors open and peeling paint, to the right a garage with a taupe car bonnet poking out of it. Ahead was a single-storey stone building with brown-painted wooden shutters open and pinned back against the wall. In the middle of the wall was a brown-painted door with a diamond-shaped window in the top half.

A flapping noise disturbed the silence. I looked up. A large black bird had landed on the ridge of the roof, disturbing part of a terracotta tile which skittered down the roof to the ground. A bloody raven. The

French hunted them as pests, but this escapee turned its head and its eye stared straight at us. I shivered and made a silent prayer to Diana the huntress. Celcus stared up at it. I tapped his arm.

'Ignore it,' I whispered. 'We'll have to take our chances.' I pointed the tip of my finger to the house door. 'Open ground, no cover, but I'll skirt round via the barn. Wait here until I signal.'

'Better if I go, *domina*. If there's trouble, you can bring the other troops in.'

'Negative. This is my call.' I swung my leg over the wall, crouched down on the far side and waited for a couple of breaths before creeping towards the barn.

Nothing. No noise from inside, but then the walls were probably a metre thick. No sound of horses or cows, not a scratching hen. A duck quacked in the distance. Ah, the pond. No geese, thank the gods. A smell of stale hay wafted from the barn. I'd have roasted my farm manager if I'd smelt that at Castra Lucilla. But it meant nobody had been working in the barn recently. No sign of movement as far as I could see in the windows of the main house.

I tabbed over to the window, flattening myself against the wall. A couple of breaths to calm my lungs, then I peeped through the glass. Two plastic bags and a backpack on a table. In the background, a kitchen range and sink piled up with plates and pans. But no people.

I shuffled along to the next window. Voices. I took a quick look and jerked back. Gods. The light from the window fell on a figure tied to a chair. Miklós. My heart hammered and the anger rode through me in a warm surge. How dared they? A tall man stood with his back to the window, but I couldn't see anything beyond his brown belted jacket and his waving hand. I wanted to smash through the bloody window, but my logical brain knew better.

Back at the house entrance I clutched my pistol to my chest and pressed lightly at the door. To my surprise it didn't creak as I opened it a few centimetres. After waiting a couple of seconds, I pushed further and slid into the farmhouse. Immediately to my left was an open doorway and then two others directly in line. No passageway or corridor, just one room leading to the next in succession.

In one step I was across the gap and hovering by a dark wooden dresser, careful not to disturb the dusty plates. I peered round the doorway. The voices were more distinct, arguing. One was shouting.

Not Miklós. The other one I knew but couldn't place it. Well, I wouldn't find out anything skulking in the kitchen. I eased round the doorway into the next room, a sitting room with old chairs and a low table with a half-filled ashtray.

'You can't keep me here, you know. They'll come for me.' Miklós's voice, tired but clear, thank the gods.

'She won't let you rot. As soon as I hear she's back home, we'll let you go,' the other one, younger, replied.

He meant me.

I heard Miklós snort.

'Oh, please! You think I believe that? Aurelia Mitela is a Roma Novan. They *never* give in to blackmail. They *never* pay ransoms.'

'But she'll make an exception for you,' the voice replied.

'No, Tom, you delude yourself,' Miklós said in a flat voice. 'She's as hard as any of them.'

Thanks, Miklós.

Then I realised what he'd said. Tom! Pluto. Tom Carter? I pulled back from the doorway and put out a hand on one of the chairs to steady myself. How in Hades was he involved?

'Are you going to bet your life on it then, Miklós?' the other voice came again.

'I wouldn't give you the odds,' my heart's love replied.

I looked round the corner again and saw that the taller figure looming over Miklós was waving a pistol in his face. Mars' balls, it *was* Tom. The widow's peak of blond hair reflected in the light from the window as he moved. Two seconds max to get to him and disarm him. I shifted my weight onto the balls of my feet ready to launch myself when cold steel jabbed my neck.

'Not so fast, darlin',' a voice said, followed by a vicious kick in the back of my knee. I gasped as my knee gave way. The steel pushed further into my flesh. A gun barrel. 'Drop the gun. Hands on your head and don't try anything clever or I'll kick your arse so hard you won't be no use to anybody.' He heaved me round.

Casely. The thug I'd disarmed in London.

15

'Happy to see me again, are we?' Casely said. Without waiting for an answer, he thrust my pistol into his pocket and shoved me through the door. I shot out my arms to keep my balance. Tom and Miklós turned and stared as I stumbled in, their arguing suspended. Miklós closed his eyes for an instant, then looked at me. Hope, concern and anger flitted across his face.

'Why are you here, Aurelia?' he said in a low voice.

'*Mußt Du das fragen?*' I murmured.

'English!' Casely growled and jabbed his pistol in my neck in the same place.

'Relax, John,' Tom said. 'She only asked him if he needed to ask.' He looked at me. 'I knew you'd come. You'd never leave him. Bit of an Achilles heel for you, isn't he?'

Tom's face didn't quite sneer, but his voice was bitter. Harry, his father, loved him unconditionally, but I'd never been sure Tom reciprocated. Now, the son seemed isolated in his own alien, unloving world. As he was still aiming a gun at Miklós's head, I wasn't going to provoke him along those lines. But I'd do anything to save my own love.

'Yes, on both counts,' I said. 'But I never expected to see you here, Tom. What on earth are you doing kidnapping Miklós? And how can you be mixed up with scum like Casely?'

A punch to my kidneys. Pain rocketed through me and I fell to my knees, gasping.

Casely shoved the barrel of his pistol under my chin, forcing my head up. His eyes shone with malice.

'Nobody bad-mouths Caselys. Your little girlie found that out when she ratted on my Linda at that fancy school.'

'Back off, John,' Tom snapped. 'Now.' His voice was cool, but there was no doubting its force. I waited, catching my breath. After a full minute, Casely took a step back from me.

'Stand up, Aurelia,' Tom said. I looked up at him, but I couldn't read the expression in his half-closed eyes as I got to my feet. Pain shot through my lower back as I moved. I pulled my lips tight together to stop myself from crying out. 'Now,' Tom continued, 'I suggest you don't antagonise my colleague any further. You can see he has a temper.'

He leant back against the wall by the window. The pale sunlight emphasised the outline of his fine-boned face.

'Nobody expects me to do anything except be a good, weak boy, do they?' he said. 'Even when I "go off the rails", as my father's fond of saying, he always forgives me.'

'He loves you, Tom. It's that simple.'

'But not enough to spend time with me.'

'But in the holidays he took you everywhere.'

'That was guilt. Ever since my mother died, he tried to be my friend.' He snorted. 'He didn't get the message.'

'But he had to look after your mother after she'd been injured in that bomb blast.'

'Why the hell was she in Africa at all? She was supposed to be looking after me.'

Gods. An oversensitive child devastated by his mother's early death had grown into an entitled one. Losing a mother early was horrendous, something I knew about only too well. But Tom had loving grandparents and his father. Why had he thought he lacked a loving environment?

He tipped his chin up at Casely and jerked his head towards Miklós. Casely moved to the back of Miklós's chair and rested the end of his pistol barrel on the crown of Miklós's head. Tom stretched his arm out, gun in hand and aimed straight at my chest. I swallowed hard. Tom's eyes gleamed in the sunlight. 'Well, I enjoy doing this,' he said and readied his weapon.

Juno save me. But the fanatic's shine in Tom's eyes told me she couldn't. Nevertheless, I was damned if I was going to let him see my fear of the bullet that would rupture my heart. I willed myself to stay immobile.

He laughed.

'Shock you, does it? That I like killing people? Too bad.'

Despite my warm jacket, I shivered. He drew his arm back, but kept me covered. If only Casely wasn't resting the barrel of his gun on Miklós's head, his finger ready to squeeze the trigger.

'I can't believe you're responsible for the deaths in Vienna and Rome and Batavia,' I said to Tom.

'Why on earth do you think I'm not capable? God, why won't anybody take me seriously?' he shrieked.

Calm, Aurelia. Calm him.

'I apologise, Tom, if I upset you. But Miklós and I have always thought a great deal of you.' I saw Miklós about to intervene, but I flicked my fingers to the floor. He sat back and watched me, his eyes half closed. 'We loved the time you visited us in Roma Nova at the farm,' I continued. 'I thought you were very happy among the horses.'

'A horse boy! Is that what you thought?' He paused for a second or two and looked across the room at nothing in particular. 'That was then.'

'Let Miklós go, Tom. He's your friend. You've shared so much. You can't want to harm him. Your quarrel is with me.'

'Quarrel? I gave you your chance in Rome to back off. But you didn't take the hint, did you?' He glanced over in Casely's direction. 'John wanted to finish you and chuck your body in the Tiber.'

I bet he did.

'You can't carry on, Tom. Even if you kill me now, others will follow.'

'I'm sure you didn't come alone to find me,' he said. 'You probably have a full special operations team surrounding the place. I'm also pretty sure they won't let me kill you in front of them. Afterwards is another matter.'

He turned to Casely.

'Untie Farkas from the chair but secure his hands behind him.

You,' he jabbed his gun at me, 'you're going to walk out of here slowly, just in front of me. Any funny business, John will shoot Miklós. Understand?'

He still couldn't bring himself to terminate Miklós himself. Some room for manoeuvre. I shrugged with my hands wide and as I brought my hands back down to my sides I brushed the radio in my pocket. I coughed loudly, hoping to mask the buzz of the signal. A tiny movement at the window like a bird's wing flapping, but I knew it would be Celcus. He was diplo protection, so trained in hostage recovery.

'I'll cooperate,' I said. 'I'll stand the others down, but please let Miklós go first,' I added in what I hoped was a firm tone. My insides were shredding with tension. Would Tom do it?

'Oh, please! Don't try that amateur bargaining on me. If I let him go, you'll try some of your heroics. Now tell your people to back off.'

Pluto in Tartarus. I shrugged again, but without touching the radio. I didn't want the rest of them charging in yet. Please Mars, Celcus was ready and Morin had his brain engaged.

'Very well,' I said, looking down. 'I need to get my radio from my pocket.'

'Slowly. Very slowly,' Tom said and fixed his stare on my left hand as I dug my fingers into my pocket. I pulled out the transceiver and flicked the transmit switch.

'Mitela to all units. Stand down. Codeword Mercury.' For the deceiver god.

The radio crackled.

'Mercury One. Understood.' Celcus, in a low voice.

'*Reçu*, Mercury Two *aussi*,' Morin.

Nothing from the third pair. Was that good or bad?

'Right, out we go,' Tom said, and jerked his gun in the direction of the doorway leading to the kitchen. There, he pointed at the external door. 'Remember what I said – no funny business. Open the door.'

I nodded. I turned the handle and stepped out into the yard. Tom was right behind me, then Miklós and Casely. On my third pace, I felt the rush of a movement and a grunt. Casely down. *Macte*, Celcus!

I spun round, brought my two fists together and knocked Tom's pistol from his hand before he could react. I kicked him hard in the groin. He grunted, gasped for breath and staggered away. I went to bodyslam him when a bullet sang through the air inches from my head. I hit the ground and pressed myself against the wall.

Hades. Pains shot through my lower back from Casely's earlier vicious punch. I grabbed some quick breaths.

A second round from an attic window, then a third, centimetres from my toes. Hugging the wall, I peeked up. The slicked back greasy hair, the grey coat collar, the hard stare. Gods, Raincoat Man from London. He'd been Tom's messenger even then.

I glanced at Celcus. He was crouching against the wall – one knee down in the centre of the unconscious Casely's back – and sawing through the rope around Miklós's wrists with his knife. Celcus paused to rifle in Casely's jacket pocket. He fished out my pistol and thrust it at me.

'Covering fire,' I whispered. Celcus nodded at me, pulled out his own pistol and half twisted in the direction of the overhead shooter.

Tom had staggered across the yard towards the garage. Sunlight flashed on the car windscreen as he flung open the driver's door. I ran after him, zigzagging as bullets danced round me, making mini-geysers of dust. What the Hades was Celcus doing? I ran for the shelter of a lean-to and caught air into my lungs. My heart was thumping. In the garage the car's engine started.

Shifting to a crouch, I readied myself to launch at the passenger side as the vehicle exited the garage and wrench the door open. But a figure flung past me. Miklós. His hands now free, he was sprinting towards the car, a fierce look like a predatory eagle on his face. Gunshots. Miklós fell in front of the car now moving forward. Oh gods. Tom wasn't going to stop.

No.

More gunshots, but no shower of bullets. I didn't care. I ran towards Miklós's slumped figure, grabbed him under the arms and started pulling him out of the path of Tom's car. Oh gods. My back was on fire, my arms weakened by the pain coursing through me. Miklós was slim, but muscled. I kept dragging. The vehicle shot out of the garage. I fell backwards as I gave one last tug. Dust exploded in clouds as the tyres screeched across the yard and the car disappeared through the gate. I thumped my transceiver twice.

I knelt over Miklós and ripped open the top of his shirt. His skin was warm, his pulse solid. Thank every god on Olympus. He groaned.

'Flesh wound,' he whispered. 'My thigh. Nothing. Go, go after him.'

'Go, major,' Celcus said. 'I'll order casevac.' He glanced up at the first floor window of the house. 'The other one's dead.'

Morin ran into the yard.

'We tried, but he drives like a demon,' he panted. 'He knocked Duvalier over as the fool stood in the middle of the road to stop him. He's okay, bruised, but okay. Duvalier, I mean.' He grabbed another breath. 'That bastard won't get far. We blew both his windscreens out. I've put out a general and immediate alert. We'll have him within the next twenty-four hours.'

16

But Morin's prophecy didn't come true. Despite a national alert, including at every frontier post and emergency circulation through every channel of the security and law enforcement agencies in France, no trace of Tom emerged. Not even a hint or sighting or a whisper. He'd simply vanished.

'I understand how frustrating it must be, *drágám,*' Miklós whispered as he leant towards me in the aeroplane. 'But you have done your very best. Even Plico must see that.'

I rubbed an imaginary smear on the Air Roma Nova plane window next to my seat and stared at the mountains below. I shifted in my seat to ease my back. The pain relief injection the Paris *medicus* had given me was wearing off. I swallowed two follow-on painkillers with a glass of water.

Plico *had* commended me when I'd reported to him on the Paris legation video link, but I'd seen that air of covering up disappointment on his face. He'd also accepted that Miklós had been duped, then drugged in London and flown to France strapped in on a supposed ambulance jet. I took Miklós's hand in mine and held it to my cheek. He seemed a little warmer than usual as if he was running a slight fever.

'You are so good for me,' I said, then smiled. 'How's the leg?'

'Itchy, but it will heal well.' His long curls brushed my cheek as he bent over and kissed me lightly.

'I still feel we've failed somehow with Tom,' I said a few minutes later. 'You could see Harry's love for him every time he looked at him. He gave Tom everything, took him to some wonderful places. And you know how responsive and open Tom was with us in Roma Nova. What in Hades happened? And how in Pluto's name am I going to tell Harry?'

Miklós pressed my hand.

'You'll find a way,' he replied and smiled at me. 'You have the strength.'

Gods, I was so lucky to have this man by my side.

The aeroplane engine roar became lighter and my ears popped as we descended into Portus Airport. Home at last and perhaps some peace.

'Mama!'

Marina rushed into my arms the minute the front door opened. I dropped to my knees and gathered her up close to me. 'Are you home properly now?' She looked straight at me, determined for an equally straight reply. At moments like this I saw a hint of Felicia, my mother, in my daughter.

'Yes, we've been away too long.' I stood and took her hand. 'Let's get some tea and you can tell me all about what you've been up to.' A small black and white ball of energy on four legs ran from the atrium into the vestibule and skidded to a halt. 'And how is Issa?' I said and bent down and stroked the small dog's head.

After a morning catching up with my assistant, Paulinus Axius, I compiled the formal report for Plico, who read it, grunted and marked it for circulation to the Joint European Liaison and Reporting Committee. Case closed.

I sent messages to Major Pirozzi, *Oberleutnant* Hartl and Agent Morin thanking them for their cooperation; Axius did the same for his Batavian colleague. And I wrote a private note to David Soane in Vienna.

The alert for Tom would stay on every law enforcement file throughout Europe. We'd circulated it to agencies across the water in the Eastern United States, Canada, in the French provinces of Quebec and Louisiana and even to the Spanish imperial viceroy's office in San Francisco. However, in the natural way of things, if nothing happened in the next few weeks, the file would be shelved and Tom's image would make its way further down in trays and be filed away under 'No further action'.

'I'll ensure they don't bury this too deep,' Axius said in our little foreign ministry office as we cleared the paperwork into archive boxes two days later. 'It'll be marked for review in three months, but I'll have another look in a few weeks' time anyway.'

'That's very good of you, Axius, but don't let it interfere with your new posting.' I would miss him, even though we'd only worked on this one project. 'Where are they sending you next?'

'I've asked to stay as liaison to the JELRC, but that's only occasional. I have the personnel interview next week.' He made a face. 'I just hope it's not some dead end analysing paperclip use.'

'That would be ridiculous,' I retorted.

'I was only joking, *domina*.' He grinned at me. 'But I hope it's something interesting.'

My own work went back to Senate committees – very uninteresting; departmental meetings – equally uninteresting; and time with Marina, which was utterly absorbing. Miklós, anxious for his horses, went out to Castra Lucilla as soon as his wound had healed.

Major Pirozzi phoned me from Rome to let me know Agent Bianchi had been dismissed from state service. Although the surveillance on him and examination of his bank account showed he'd been taking bribes, nothing could prove any connection to the Italian deputy minister's murder.

'Any progress on that?' I asked.

'Only speculation so far,' he said, then paused.

'Such as?'

'*Allora*, the latest theory is that he was going to rat on his criminal colleagues so they silenced him by putting out a contract to a hit man.'

Tom.

Licinia sent a confidential telex from the Vienna legation with Hartl's thoughts about Teiderstein's killing.

LEG.VINDOBONA 09NOV1974 1512
CELATA
FOR MITELA
VICTIM HEAVILY INVOLVED PROPERTY SPECULATION AND POSSIBLE CRIMINAL USE OF SUCH PROPERTY. LINKS TO ORG CRIME. POSSIBLY DEFAULTING ON PAYMENTS, HENCE CONTRACT KILLING. INVESTIGATION CONTINUES.
ENDS

Harry Carter arrived at Portus Airport a few days later at my invitation. I wasn't sure he'd come. When I saw how tired he looked as he trudged down the plane steps, my heart sank.

'Hello, Aurelia. Kind of you to invite me.' He wiped his fingers across his forehead. 'If nothing else, I could do with a break from fending off the tabloids.'

'Do you know who leaked the story about Tom to the press?'

'I was rather hoping you might know.' His voice was bitter, almost accusing.

'Be assured, Harry, it wasn't from the Roma Nova side. The whole operation was tagged highly confidential.'

He said nothing but just sank back into the car seat as we drove into the city. Thirty minutes later we were at Domus Mitelarum and sitting in the atrium corner. I handed him a whisky.

'We can talk tonight or wait until tomorrow,' I started. 'I think you might like to rest first, but it's up to you.'

He took a good sip of his whisky. His fair hair, growing in that same distinctive widow's peak I'd last seen on Tom, looked lank. Purple shadows bloomed under his eyes.

'I know the basics, of course,' he said, looking into his glass. 'But I'd be glad of the detail from the source.'

'Then we'll go to my office in the morning and you can read the whole file.'

I instructed my steward to put Harry in a room at the back overlooking the garden and the park beyond and gave strict orders for silence from the staff in the area. When I returned from my run in the parkland at seven the next morning, I was unhappy to see Harry in a chair on the patio, smoking.

'That's new, isn't it?' I said pointing to the cigarette.

He threw it on the patio and stubbed it out with his foot.

'Bloody things, but they have a calming effect,' he replied. 'I thought you were still in bed and I could sneak down before breakfast.' He gave a rueful smile like a schoolboy caught smoking in the lavatory. But it was good to see a smile from him.

Plico was all politeness which was unnerving, but he seemed genuinely pleased to see Harry. Heads of spook services seemed to have an automatic, if slightly wary, camaraderie.

'I'm deeply grateful for everything that Aurelia has done and, of course, for your support,' Harry told Plico. 'I know she was as shocked as I was to discover Tom had become enmeshed in this business.'

I said nothing but sat unmoving in the second chair on the far side of Plico's desk. 'Enmeshed in this business' was not how I would have described Tom's becoming a professional assassin. It wasn't business; it was murder.

'She'll show you everything we've been able to do,' Plico said, as if I wasn't in the room. 'However, we can't commit any further resources unless anything else comes up. The alerts will stay live for at least another six months. After that...' Plico shrugged. 'I'm only sorry we haven't come up with a better result for you or for us.'

'I completely understand, Secretary Plico,' Harry said a little stiffly. 'You'll let me know, I presume, if there are any developments your end?'

'Of course,' Plico replied in his smoothest tone, then rose and held out his hand. We were dismissed.

Along the service corridors, builders in overalls and protective hats were fixing cables, plastering and doing what builders did. Dust floated in the air along with the smells of sweat, paint and concrete.

'I do apologise for making you walk through a building site, Harry, but we're nearly there.'

'Don't worry, please. It's a relief to see other people in a mess.'

I didn't think he meant the building.

I closed the small window in my office to shut out the noise. When I turned to speak to Harry, he was wiping away a tear and sniffed loudly into a white cotton handkerchief.

'Harry…'

'No, I'm sorry. I didn't mean to lose control. How embarrassing.'

'My dear, you're perfectly entitled to do so.'

'How the hell did he turn into this monster? I just don't recognise my son in this… this killer. I've obviously cocked up somewhere.'

'No, you've been a good father. Sometimes people born with personal gifts and given every opportunity still turn out badly. Or worse.' I wasn't going to throw Caius Tellus at him, but that manipulative bastard and Tom both demonstrated the arrogant belief they were entitled to trample ruthlessly over people's lives.

'What would happen if in the future you *did* track him down?' Harry's voice was tight and he swallowed hard.

'We'd put him on trial here and he'd be sentenced accordingly.'

Harry's shoulders slumped.

'We couldn't let him go, Harry,' I said as gently as I could.

'No, I don't suppose you could. But he'd wither in a tough prison.'

'We don't ill-treat prisoners, you know,' I replied. What had he expected? 'I'm sorry, Harry, but he has murdered and kidnapped his way across Europe. He intended to terminate me and Miklós.'

'But he was desperate to escape.' His eyes pleaded.

'No, he kidnapped Miklós to entrap me because I was investigating his murders and closing in on him.' Harry flinched. I nearly didn't continue, but Harry had to accept how Tom was now, how beyond the pale his actions were. 'And Tom spoke of the satisfaction he experienced when he killed. If we find him, he will receive counselling and therapy along with his imprisonment. We can do nothing less. But nothing more.'

I walked back to the entrance hall of the foreign ministry in silence with the man whose heart was not only broken but whose soul was now filled with the lead of despair. In the vestibule, Harry shook my hand.

'I'm grateful, Aurelia, for what you've done, and I accept what you've said about Tom. And I'm desperately sorry for what he did to you and Miklós, but against all my principles, deep in my heart, I hope you never find him.'

17

Three weeks later, I was sweating over a strategy review of our legation network and which ones we could afford to cut, or at least where we could reduce staffing. Imperatrix Justina had been strongly lobbied in the imperial council by the interior minister demanding more funding for the *vigiles*. An injection of significant funding would increase their crime clear-up rate exponentially, he'd insisted; that was all that was hindering them. I'd seen communal litter-picking better organised and more effective than our police forces. They were poorly motivated and lazy in my opinion, and too many of them were overweight.

But he'd attacked our foreign representation, slicing away at the rationale and cost of why a small country like Roma Nova needed such a large diplomatic network. Hades damn him. Hadn't he read any history? By gathering secrets and using influence that network had been vital to Roma Nova's survival through the ages.

I had to get the damn riposte ready for the next imperial council meeting, the last before Saturnalia, thank the gods.

I was scratching in red pen over my first draft, recalculating a complex row of figures when the shrill ring of my phone interrupted me. I jabbed the calculating machine to 'Off' and picked up the handset.

'Mitela.'

'Plico. In my office, now.'

Gods, what had happened?

On the third floor, Plico's assistant waved me in without a word.

'Read this,' he said as I was sitting down and half threw a telex printout at me.

LEG.VINDOBONA 13DEC1974 1038
CELATA
FOR PLICO, MITELA
UNCONFIRMED SIGHTING OF T.CARTER AT WIEN SÜDBAHNHOF.
EXACT DESTINATION UNKNOWN. NEW AUSTRIAN GENDARMERIE PURSUING ENQUIRIES
LICINIA

I glanced at my watch. The telex had been sent forty minutes ago. I was on my feet, ready to go.

'Wait,' Plico growled. 'Licinia's sound, isn't she?'

'Completely, and she will have had this direct from Hartl, the *Gendarmerie* lieutenant who was our liaison.'

'Oh?'

'They're social partners.'

'How convenient.' He smirked. 'Never mind that. Get on the video link and see if there's anything else she can tell you.'

'One thing,' I said. 'The main line from the Südbahnhof goes south-west to Klagenfurt, but also to Graz for the direct services into Roma Nova.'

'Hartl's already on it, major,' Licinia said from the black and white screen. 'He's alerted his colleagues in Klagenfurt. They'll keep a continuous watch on the Vienna trains for the next forty-eight hours. He's sent out plainclothes to Graz town, to the railway station there and, just as a precaution, to the car hire firms. And, of course, to the frontier with Roma Nova. He's also tipped off airport security just in case.'

'I expected no less. He struck me as very efficient.'

Licinia didn't quite give a smile, but her formal professional face relaxed a minim.

'He's still getting a lot of political pressure to clear up the Teiderstein murder,' she continued. 'A fresh lead is a relief. The New Austrian border police will carry out a full check on all male passengers on the trains going into Roma Nova—'

'Ask Hartl not to make it too officious. If it *is* Tom Carter, I'd prefer to catch him our side of the border.'

She hesitated.

'Hartl would like to arrest him here so he can get the politicos off his back.'

'I understand, Licinia, but ask Hartl if he has a completely unassailable audit trail of evidence, one that will lead to an assured conviction. Here, I can give personal witness testimony that will convict him under the Paris Convention.' I looked directly at her. 'You know your duty.'

'Of course, major. There is no need to remind me,' she said huffily. 'Licinia out.'

My PGSF snatch squad was littered around the main platform of the Roma Nova Interrail station, disguised as cleaners, railway staff and passengers. When I'd briefed them with the background and objective of the operation, their faces became grimmer.

'So as the target is a known killer, I take it we have the usual permission to terminate, if necessary, ma'am?' the older of the two *optio*s asked.

'No!'

Gods. Not Tom. How could I face Harry afterwards? The *optio* raised an eyebrow at my answer. Damn, I'd been out of this too long. Standing orders gave permission as a default; PGSF were trained to make judgements in the middle of live operations. What was I thinking of? I cleared my throat.

'My mistake, *optio*. But only if you consider your life or the lives of others is in danger. And only then. Understood?'

He nodded, but I noticed he exchanged glances with the other *optio*.

• • •

A bleak December wind blew across the platform. I pulled my wool hat down to meet the scarf around my neck and huddled behind a newspaper I was pretending to read. Only three high-speed direct trains were scheduled from Vienna today and this was the first since the alert from Licinia. I could have left it to the troops, but I had a deep personal interest in catching Tom; not because of the international killings, nor my wish to help Harry. No, it was his attack on Miklós who'd befriended him. That betrayal stung me more openly than it seemed to have Miklós. But although he appeared to accept it as another of life's nasty surprises, I thought that underneath he *was* deeply affected.

Plico hadn't even tried to stop me coming here; I would have come anyway, and he knew it. He saved face by saying that as I could identify the target without question, he would allow me to lead the operation.

A yellow engineering maintenance engine chuntered through, emitting diesel fumes and noise. I checked my watch. Five minutes to go. Stopping only at Graz on its way from Vienna and then the border with Roma Nova, this train terminated here. It would disgorge its passengers on this platform. Hartl's people had recorded no sightings at the border, but we wouldn't let it rest there.

A buzz on my radio. The red and white engine of the *Neuösterreichische Staatsbahn* was crawling towards us. It ground to a stop amidst screeching brakes. Doors swung open from its four passenger carriages. We could be looking at two hundred people, but only about half of that number stepped out. Some were women with children, the usual business types, some students, tourists heaving cases down, three fashionable young women accompanied by a camera crew with large black boxes on a hand wagon, and obvious hikers with backpacks and mountain gear.

I scrutinised the single young men carefully, but wondered if Tom would be that obvious. None had his slim build or fair hair, but those were things that could be easily disguised. Tom had one obvious trait; he walked with a long loping gait, something that would be hard to alter. But I couldn't see anybody walking that way or unnaturally or limping to disguise it. Within three minutes, every passenger had disappeared from the platform.

Hades.

We'd have to wait for the afternoon train, and it had just begun to sleet. But first we needed to carry out a full search of this train, empty or not.

'Aquila Zero to all units. Report only if anything or anybody sighted in current location.'

No replies.

'Aquila Zero to all units,' I growled with disappointment. 'Fall back to marshalling yard for final search.' I flicked my radio off, grabbed a second carriage door and swung inside the train as it moved off.

The yard wasn't that extensive with only half a dozen sets of lines, but there were numerous sheds and stores scattered round the edges – plenty of places to hide. As the train rumbled along slowly, jerking as it crossed points, I stayed low. I could just peer out of the less than pristine window.

Then I saw it. A black blob in the sky, beating large wings. I couldn't hear its raucous shriek, but I knew it was a raven. It landed on a stationary carriage, ignoring the sleet. My logical brain told me it was coincidence, but something deep in my Roman blood crawled at the thought of this unlucky harbinger here, now.

Figures, human ones, were spreading across the railway yard, jumping rails. My detail. I blinked and the raven had gone. Thank Diana. Small groups of disguised PGSF clambered on each end of the train. They'd work methodically through the train to the middle. Others would search on top and underneath. And we'd do the same for every train until we caught him.

I pulled my pistol out of its holster and held it close to my chest. If the searchers flushed Tom out, he'd run either out into the yards where others would have him or along the train where I would be waiting.

Five minutes passed. I heard doors slamming, shouting footfall, the rattle of a service cart, a voice in Germanic raised in protest. Damn, some of the train crew were still on board. But the troops would send the New Austrians back behind them as they came forward in their search. Despite the heating turned off, the carriage was still warm from the departed passengers. A newspaper lay abandoned on a seat.

Were we wasting our time? Well, if it was a no show, we'd finish here and return in two hours' time and repeat everything. I stood up and raised my radio to my lips.

The doors of the next carriage slammed. A figure burst through the black rubber concertina of the gangway connector.

Tom.

'Halt!' I shouted and raised my arm. He stopped in mid stride and stared at the pistol in my hand. 'Stand completely still, Tom. Arms away from your body.'

He blinked, then complied.

'Sit over by the window where you can be seen, knees apart and place your hands on your head. And please don't try anything silly or I will shoot you.'

'Think you've got me, don't you?' His eyes gleamed.

'I do seem to have the advantage.'

My radio buzzed.

'Aquila Zero,' I replied.

'Negative report.'

'Aquila Zero. I have him. Carriage 2. Send a guard to each end interior and exterior.'

'Aquila One. Understood. Out.'

I watched as a guard appeared through the connecting gangway each end. Both carried service pistols; the younger one also a rifle slung diagonally over her shoulder. Now I holstered my own weapon and sat diagonally across from Tom.

'Two things. Firstly, you may place your hands on your knees. Do not move beyond that – the consequences will be extremely uncomfortable for you. Secondly, I want to know why you think you are entitled to go on a killing spree round Europe.'

Sleet battered on the window, but Tom's face looked bleaker than the sky it was falling from.

'You don't understand. Nor will you.'

'Oh, please,' I said and flicked my fingers. 'You sound like something from a bad film. Was it money? Or the thrill?'

'You don't have a clue, Aurelia.'

'I hope not. I'm waiting for you to enlighten me.'

'You had a privileged upbringing—'

'So did you. Next.'

'Your mother was there all the time.'

'No, she worked. I had no father, unlike you. And a better father than Harry would be hard to find.'

'As I said, you don't get it.'

'Stop making dramatic non-statements and tell me straight.'

'What do you think it's like being at school and the others knowing you're a spook's child? The school bully beating you to get you to tell secrets? Then his friends holding you down while he buggered you. They took photos telling me they'd send them to the papers. I was fifteen, for Christ's sake.'

'Oh, Tom. You should have told your father.'

'No! I was too embarrassed. He'd have raised a massive stink. I found another way. Nobody ever knew the cause of the tragic accident of Anderson's death. Only that he fell in the school lake and drowned. My first.' He leant back completely relaxed as if he'd achieved something satisfactory.

Gods.

'You know that was wrong, don't you, Tom?'

'No, it was justice. He was a bastard and deserved it. You have restorative justice here. You understand. You're a Roman.'

He leant forward. One of the guards raised his weapon in Tom's direction. It was the older *optio* from the briefing. I held my hand up and he relaxed.

'Sit back, Tom.'

He did, a half-smile on his lips.

'I found I had a talent for it and certain people became interested in my talent. Besides, I liked it. For once, I had control of what was happening.'

'Did you feel no pity for the people you murdered?'

'Murdered? No, executed. A child trafficker, a money launderer of funds from prostitution and a vicious pornographer? Scum, all three.' He snorted.

'There are judicial procedures, you know. You would have been better helping the authorities find evidence to convict them.'

He laughed.

'And have them bribe their way out? No. Much more fun to kill them.'

What was this monster in front of me? I swallowed to stop a sour taste rising in my gullet.

'Why are you in Roma Nova, Tom?'

He looked away and even in this poor light, I saw the colour in his face deepen.

'You have no quarrel with Miklós,' I said. 'You can't have come after him.'

'God, no, but it will cause him pain.' He turned back and gave me a knowing look. A smile formed on his lips.

Juno, it was me. He'd come to terminate me. I tried to ignore the hammering in my heart. Calm. I had to stay calm.

'They would have come after you, if you'd succeeded,' I said in as firm a voice as I could muster.

'Possibly, but would they have been as determined?' His smile dropped and he glared at me. 'You stopped me. People wouldn't give me another contract once they heard you were after me.' His eyes bored into mine. 'My father likes and respects you, but I hate you.' And it did seem as if something black and vicious flowed from him. 'I'd finish you in a second.'

I stood. I'd had enough of this.

'I have no interest in your hatred,' I said. 'Now you're going to face justice yourself – my attempted murder and kidnapping Miklós to start with. Then we'll find the evidence trail to the other Europeans.' I flicked my hand upwards. 'Stand up and turn round. Hands behind your back.' I signalled to one of the guards to give me a pair of handcuffs. As I stretched out my hand to receive them, Tom bodyslammed me. The *optio* raised his pistol to shoot, but Tom had heaved open the carriage door and jumped out as the shot rang over his head.

I scrambled up, gasping to recover my wind.

'Get after him,' I shouted out of the door. The two guards outside ran after the figure zigzagging across the yard. The guards inside with me moved to the door to join them, but I held my hand out. I looked at the younger one carrying the rifle. A sniper rifle complete with telescopic sight.

'Team markswoman, I presume?'

'Yes, ma'am,' she piped up. Now I saw her earnest face, I wondered how much over sixteen she was.

'Can you bring him down?'

'Yes.'

She perched on the seat, smashed the small passenger window and rested her weapon on the edge. As she was sighting on her target, the *optio*, who must have been twice her age, bent down and whispered in her ear. She glanced up at him and frowned. He nodded. She shot.

18

I clambered down and raced across the tracks to where Tom had fallen. I dropped down and ripped open his jacket. A dark stain bloomed on his pale blue jumper. His pulse was faint, irregular.

'Medivac. Stat!' I shouted.

A figure with the twin snakes of Asclepius on his armband knelt beside me. He carried out vital signs check, looked at me and shook his head.

Tom's lips moved and I bent down.

'You win, Aurelia,' he said. 'Tell Pa I'm sorry.' Then he sighed out of life.

I brought my hands up to my face and sobbed; for the waste of a young life twisted out of true, and for his father whose heart would break a second time.

At PGSF headquarters, the young markswoman stood stiffly in front of me. She was trembling.

'I know he was moving, young woman,' I said in the iciest voice possible, 'but you should have been able to make a disabling shot only. I suggest you take a remedial course on target shooting. And I recommend a parallel study of Pelantius's *Ethics of War*. Now get out.'

She made the fastest exit I'd seen in a long time. The *optio* was an entirely different matter.

'How long have you been a Praetorian?'

'Twelve years, ma'am.'

I looked at his file which I'd requested from the adjutant. The *optio*'s commendations were remarkable, awarded for his actions, decisiveness and cool-headedness. Except for one incident when he'd stepped over the line and been broken down from centurion.

'You're a problem for me, *optio*. You're obviously a great asset to the Guard, but inveigling a youngling to take a fatal shot is tantamount to murder.'

'I don't know what the major means,' he said looking at the wall behind me.

'Yes, you do, and don't take that insolent attitude with me. I've seen it all before.'

'The perpetrator was resisting arrest. Tertia mistimed her shot.'

'Really?' I leant back in my seat. 'What exactly did you say to her to make her frown just before she fired?'

'I reminded her to take aim carefully. She was a little resentful at my advice.'

'That's exactly what she says.'

I tapped on the desk with my pen.

'I can't take it further, but never, ever let me hear that you took such an action again.'

'Ma'am.'

'Out,' I snapped.

'You were too harsh on the man and the girl,' Miklós said as he stroked my hair that evening. He'd come straight back as soon as I'd phoned him at the farm.

'That's what Plico said. He told me not to mention it in my report. But it's not right.' I took a large swallow of my brandy. 'What in Hades am I going to tell Harry?'

'Nothing. You mustn't. Sometimes you just have to let things go. Tom was a known criminal who admitted three high-profile assassinations that we know of. True, his victims were unpleasant and involved in dirty activities themselves, so....' He shrugged and looked away.

'You're surely not condoning what he did?'

'No, of course not,' he added rather too quickly. 'But attacking you?' His expression tightened and his hold on my hand became tighter. 'Over the line.'

'I've given up counting the number of lines Tom crossed,' I said.

'Yes, but this was so personal.' Miklós was still frowning.

'Agreed, but that's what I have to deal with – occupational hazard.'

'I wish it wasn't. Can't Plico give you a desk job from now on?'

I drew back from him and sat up straight. I didn't quite glare.

'Do you honestly see me driving a desk?'

Still leaning back, half sitting, half lying in the folds of the sofa, he smiled at me.

'Not really, but it was worth a try,' he said. He pulled me to him, folded me in his arms and kissed the top of my head.

Harry arrived the next day to take his son home, but scarcely said a word beyond absolute essentials as I signed the release papers in his presence. Poor man. I grieved for him.

Miklós and I flew back to the United Kingdom a few days later for Tom's funeral when he was interred next to his mother's grave. It was a cold day, but clear and sunny, and about twenty people stood at the graveside as Harry threw a sprig of rosemary onto the coffin just before he turned away. We walked back to the cars in the burial ground car park and waited until Harry had said goodbye to the other friends and family. I hoped he would still count us as friends, but if he never wanted to speak to me or Miklós again, we would have to accept his decision.

'Harry—' I began.

'Aurelia. I'm sorry I haven't had a chance to talk to you today. Thank you for coming.' His tone was formal and weary.

'It's the least we could do. I'm so sorry it ended as it did.'

'I suppose it was inevitable.'

Gods, his voice was shorn of hope. He looked as if he wanted to escape to a dark corner and fall into it.

'He followed a tragic path,' I said after a few moments. 'But his last words were for you – "Tell Pa I'm sorry".'

Harry passed a finger across his cheek. Perhaps it was the cold, but his eyes were red and glistening.

'Very thoughtful of you to tell me that, Aurelia. Tom was a good boy at heart, a cheerful, but sensitive little soul as a child. I'll always remember him as then, not as now.' He held his hand out. 'Thank you both for the friendship you gave him when he was older. Perhaps I should have listened to you and let him stay with you in Roma Nova before he went to Cambridge.'

'Oh, Harry, don't. Don't do this to yourself.' I took his hand. 'You did your very best. None of us can make people do what we want. They have to follow their own course, whatever their start in life.'

He gave me no reply, only a little smile.

I hadn't been able to help Tom in the end. I hadn't even been able to keep him alive. But what good would it have done? Perhaps death had been a release for the desperately unhappy young man. I couldn't say more, but just gave Harry a brief hug. Miklós took Harry's arm and helped him to his car while I trailed along behind, sorrow filling my heart.

Two months later, I saw a British newspaper report about Harry. His genial face stared out from a photo featuring a group, mostly of youngsters but with three adults, one of whom was the British minister for education and training.

New Foreign Office undersecretary launches international mentoring scheme.

Mr Henry Carter has generously funded ten placements for young people from a variety of backgrounds to foster better understanding between people from different nations. Emphasis will be on building personal relationships, strengthening core values and exchanging ideas internationally. Mr Carter's son, Thomas, was tragically killed in an accident abroad. The new scheme will bear his name.

I laid the paper down and picked up my fountain pen to write Harry a note. If he agreed, Roma Nova would offer as many placements as he wished.

I showed the paper to Miklós that evening after supper.

'A good man with a faithful heart,' he said. 'I will help, of course. Perhaps some races and horse-trekking in the mountains…'

'I still wish we had been able to steer Tom back,' I said.

'You did your best, *drágám*. But you also did what was right. You will always do the right thing and you always know what that is. Roma Nova never had a truer servant, nor one with a truer heart.'

'I'm not sure about that, Miklós. I just know that we have to be ready for anything the future may throw at us.'

WOULD YOU LEAVE A REVIEW?

I hope you enjoyed NEXUS which takes place between AURELIA and INSURRECTIO in the Roma Nova series

If you did, I'd really appreciate it if you would write a few words of review on the site where you purchased this book.

Reviews help books to feature more prominently on retailer sites and let more people into the world of Roma Nova.

Very many thanks!

THE STORY BEFORE NEXUS

Read the start of AURELIA, the story of how Aurelia's military career (which she loved) was interrupted brutally and how the lifelong rivalry between her and Caius Tellus grew ever more bitter and then turned lethal...

I

I left my side arm in the safe box in the vestibule and walked on past the marble and plaster *imagines*, the painted statues and busts of Mitela ancestors from the gods knew how many hundreds of years. Only the under-steward was allowed to dust them; I'd never been permitted to touch them as a child.

My all-terrain boots made soft squelching sounds as I crossed the marble floor. This was the last private time I'd share with my mother and daughter for three weeks. A glance at my watch confirmed I had a precious hour.

Through the double doors, the atrium rose up for three storeys. Light from the late spring sun beat down through the central glass roof onto luxuriant green planting at the centre of the room like rays from an intense spotlight. My mother disliked the vastness of the atrium and had partitioned a part of it off with tall bookcases, to make a cosier area, she said. Unfortunately, because of the almost complete square of tall units with only a body-width entrance at the far corner, and the way the shelving inside was arranged, you couldn't see who was there until you were on top of them. I'd been trapped by some of my mother's tea-drinking cronies more than once.

My mother, sitting on her favourite chintz sofa facing the entrance, looked up as I appeared in the gap. Two tiny creases on her forehead vanished when she stood and walked towards me with her arms extended. She greeted me with an over-bright smile.

'Aurelia, darling.'

I bent and kissed her cheek in a formal salute then looked over her shoulder to where my daughter, Marina, was sitting quietly on the sofa. She was twisting her hands together and glancing in as many different directions as she could.

'Marina, whatever is the matter, sweetheart?' I strode over and crouched down by her. She stretched her hand out to grab mine and pointed at the chair in the far corner.

Caius Tellus.

Hades in Pluto.

'Aurelia, how lovely to see you,' he said in a warm, urbane voice.

Taller than his brother Quintus who nearly topped two metres,

Caius was well built without being overweight. Sitting at his ease, one leg crossed over the other, he ran his eyes over my face and body. His hazel eyes shone and his smile was wide, showing a glimpse of over-white teeth through generous lips. Nothing in his tanned face with classic cheekbones would repel you on the surface. Others considered him very good-looking with almost film star glamour and charm. I knew better what kind of creature lay underneath.

Even as a kid he'd had a vicious streak; I'd never forget his hand clamping my neck, forcing my face down into the scullery drain, him saying he'd drown me in filth. I'd retched and retched at the smell of animal blood, the grease and dirty water. In the end, the cook had found us and hauled Caius off. I'd crouched there sweating and trembling; only horseplay, Caius said and laughed. The cook had given him a hard look, but the other servants were won over by Caius's boyish smile. But when he'd stuck his hand up my skirt and tried to force me at Aquilia's emancipation party, I'd kneed him in the groin so hard he couldn't stand up for hours. I'd been in the military cadets for a year by then. But the others, woozy from wine and good spirits, gave him more sympathy as he writhed around on the terrace, playing to the audience.

After I joined the Guard at eighteen, I hardly saw him except at formal Twelve Families events and even there, he'd smarm his way to the head of the food queues or make a beeline for the most vulnerable in the room, be it male or female. He was a taker in life, a callous one. I loathed him with all my heart and soul.

I stood up, shielding Marina behind me.

'Dear me,' he said, 'are you off playing soldiers again?'

I should have been given top marks for not slapping the smirk off his face.

'Caius,' I said, keeping my voice as cool as possible. 'We're having a private family lunch before I go on an extended operation, so I hope you'll excuse us.'

My mother cast a pleading look at me. I closed my eyes for a second. She'd invited him to join us. How could she have?

I chewed my food slowly to try to reduce my tension. I was irritated Mama had chosen the breakfast room – a private family place – to eat in rather than the formal dining room. The servants flitted in and out with the food, and I said very little except to Marina, who ate very little.

'Aurelia, you're quieter than usual. I hope nothing's wrong?' my mother said too cheerfully.

Before I could answer, Caius intervened. 'She does look a little pale. Don't you worry, Felicia, that she takes on too much sometimes?' He tilted his head sideways and pasted a concerned expression onto his face.

I speared a piece of pork and sawed through it like a barbarian, scraping the plate glaze below. I knew Caius was trying to make me rise to his bait, but I refused to play. At least my work as a Praetorian soldier was serving the state. He served himself with his gambling and whoring. He put in just enough hours at the charity committees he nominally sat on to appear to be contributing to Roma Novan life.

My mother smiled at him. 'Yes, I do wonder. She was so exhausted after that last exercise abroad. You really understand, don't you, Caius?'

He extended his hand and grasped hers and smiled. I was nearly sick.

'"She" wasn't exhausted,' I cut across. 'It was food poisoning, as you know very well, Mama. And it was all over within thirty-six hours.'

Caius smiled at me this time, but it didn't reach his eyes. 'Your mother's right, you know. You have a duty to look after your rather, er, small family.'

I stood up and threw my napkin on the table.

'The day I need you to teach me my duty doesn't exist, Caius. Keep your nose out of my family affairs.' I held my hand out to Marina, but fixed my gaze on my mother's face. 'I'm sure Nonna will allow you to leave the table now, Marina. We're going for a walk outside in the fresh air.'

My mother gave a brief nod. I caught Caius's second smirk out of the corner of my eye. One of these days...

Marina and I crossed the terrace and wound through the formal parterres and reached the swings at the side.

'Nonna wants me to be friends with Caius Tellus,' she said, 'but I don't like him. He makes me feel funny.' I hugged her to me. She was so fragile; fine red-brown hair and a delicate face, light brown eyes like a frightened rabbit, not the bright Mitela blue like mine and my mother's. Never robust, Marina had coughed and wheezed her way through infancy, floored by the least infection.

My heart constricted as I recalled yet again that terrible day when she was just two. I'd rushed back, heart pounding, from the training ground. Still in my dusty green and brown combats, I'd stared down at my daughter; white, inanimate. I'd dropped to my knees and touched her forehead. Damp, cold, sweating. Her hand was equally chill. The nurse had wrapped her in light wool blankets and bonnet to prevent body heat loss and a drip line ran from her nostril up to a suspended plastic bag on a steel stand. I was a major in the Praetorian Guard and commanded some of the toughest soldiers in Roma Nova with the most modern weaponry on the entire planet, but I'd never felt more powerless.

Now I had to protect her against a subtler virus.

'You don't have to be friends with anybody you don't want to, whatever anybody says – me and Nonna included.'

'But Nonna said it was important. I have to get used to it for when he comes to live in our house.'

I stared at Marina. What in Hades was my mother hatching up now? All I could hear was an angry buzz in my head, soaring to deafening levels. Marina's face tightened. She dropped my hand and shrank back.

'It's all right, darling. I'm sorry, I didn't mean to scare you.' I swallowed hard. 'I was a bit surprised, that's all.' I delayed, struggling to keep my temper and not frighten my soft child. 'When did Nonna say that?'

'Before lunch.' She dropped her gaze to the ground.

I crouched down in front of her and touched her cheek.

'Look at me, Marina. I promise you here and now that I will never be friends with Caius Tellus. He will not come and live with me. If Nonna invites him, you and I will go and live on the farm together.'

She lifted her head, two tiny wet streaks on her cheeks.

'Cross your heart?'

'And hope to die in the arena.'

Caius was drinking coffee with my mother when I returned alone to the atrium. He gave a knowing little smile when I requested an urgent private word with my mother. We walked in silence to an unused office at the back of the house. Its virtue was that it was part of the ancient building and had very thick walls.

'What the hell are you playing at?' I said. 'And how in Hades do you think you have the right to pressure my five-year-old child to cosy up to that slimy bastard Caius?'

I stood a body-length away from my mother, further than my fists could reach.

'Don't use your rough soldier's language with me, my girl. I've dropped enough hints over the past year, but you've been ignoring them. You need another child. As insurance.'

'I hope you're not serious, Mama.'

'You have responsibilities. House Mitela needs heirs and Marina isn't strong.'

I stared at her for a full minute.

'I'm twenty-eight – not exactly past it,' I said. 'And I have two male cousins in the first degree.'

'Neither of whom could inherit except by imperial decree. That hasn't happened to the Mitelae yet. And Imperatrix Justina would be hard to persuade on this. Take my word for it.'

'She can't insist.'

'No, but she'd speak about duty and history and make you feel like a shirker.'

'For Juno's sake, it's the nineteen sixties. I'm not a breeding filly.'

'No, but you are the heir to the senior of the Twelve Families whose sworn duty is to support the Apulian imperatrix and the continued existence of Roma Nova. Caius is an ideal prospect, personable and intelligent. He belongs to a good family that has been allied to ours for over fifteen hundred years.'

'Don't hide behind history, Mama. I know what you're up to and the answer's no. Not a hope. Ever.'

'What's wrong with him? I know you didn't get on very well with him as children, but you've grown out that awkward stage. You're an adult now. Old Countess Tella would be pleased for an alliance with our family.'

No doubt Caius's great-aunt would be thrilled. I was the bait for every other one of the Twelve. But I would choose my partner myself, not submit to some old girls' cosy arrangement. I'd already had the dubious pleasure of one unsatisfactory companion in Marina's father; I didn't want a second one.

'If you don't get it, Mama, I don't know where to start. Can't you see how manipulative Caius is? He's flashed his teeth at you, said a few smarmy phrases to lure you onto his side. Now he has you trying to finesse Marina.' I snorted. 'Look at his eyes sometime when he's not trying to charm you. He's mean and cruel. Ask his brother Quintus.' I glanced at my watch. 'I have to go now.'

'Won't you even talk to him?'

'No. My mind's made up. There is no more discussion.'

'Well, have a think about it while you're away.'

She made it sound like a holiday. We'd be freezing our arses off on a snow-covered mountain, grabbing three to four hours' sleep, either bored out of our minds or targeted by tough criminals and snipers.

'We'll talk properly when I'm back, if you insist. But I don't want Caius Tellus within fifty metres of Marina while I'm away. A hundred, preferably. Promise me that.'

Her eyes dropped under my intense stare.

'Do you promise?'

'Don't be so angry, Aurelia. I'll do as you ask. But try to calm down and think logically. You need more heirs.'

For a clever woman, my mother was sometimes so simple. I tamped down the heat of anger rushing through my body.

'Let me assure you, Mama, that even if Caius was the last man on earth, I'd rather kill myself than let him touch me.'

AURELIA is available as ebook, paperback and audiobook. See https://alison-morton.com/books-2/aurelia/ for full details.

HISTORICAL NOTE

NEXUS reveals an episode in Aurelia Mitela's life between *AURELIA* set in the late 1960s and *INSURRECTIO* in the early 1980s when everything in Roma Nova fell apart. 'Nexus' can mean connection, entwining, binding and a focal point.

Roma Nova is an imaginary country, but its roots are solidly fixed in the ancient Roman Empire at the time it was breaking up. Just suppose a small group of Romans had trekked north out of the city in those unstable times and established their own mountain colony that survived into the modern era and thrived? And suppose women, through circumstances over fifteen centuries, now ran Roma Nova?

This is speculation, but that's what alternative history fiction is all about – playing with the idea of 'what if'.

Suppose Julius Caesar had taken notice of the warning that assassins wanted to murder him on the ides of March? Suppose Elizabeth I had married and had children? If plague hadn't rampaged through Europe in the fourteenth century? Or if Christianity had remained a Middle Eastern minor cult, or Napoleon had won at Waterloo?

The concept of a society with Roman values surviving for fifteen centuries is meant to intrigue, but I have dropped background 'history' of Roma Nova into NEXUS only where it impacts on the story. Nobody likes a history lesson in the middle of a thriller! But if you are interested in how the mysterious Roma Nova survived into the twentieth century, read on...

What happened in our timeline

Our timeline may of course, turn out to be somebody else's alternative one as shown in Philip K. Dick's *The Grasshopper Lies Heavy*, the story within the story in *The Man in the High Castle*. Nothing is fixed. But for the sake of convenience I take ours as the default.

The Western Roman Empire didn't 'fall' in a cataclysmic event as often portrayed in film and television; it localised and dissolved like chain mail fragmenting into separate links, giving way to rump provinces, city states and petty kingdoms. The Eastern Roman Empire survived until the Fall of Constantinople in 1453 to the Ottoman Empire.

Some scholars think that Christianity fatally weakened the traditional Roman way of life. Emperor Constantine's personal conversion to Christianity in AD 313 was a turning point. By late AD 394, his several times successor, Theodosius, had banned all traditional Roman religious practice, closed and destroyed temples and dismissed all priests. The sacred flame that had burned in the College of Vestals for over a thousand years was extinguished and the vestal virgins expelled. The Altar of Victory, said to guard the fortune of Rome, was hauled away from the Senate building and disappeared from history.

The Roman senatorial families pleaded for religious tolerance, but Theodosius made any pagan practice, even dropping a pinch of incense on a family altar in a private home, into a capital offence. And his 'religious police', driven by the austere and ambitious bishop Ambrosius of Milan, became increasingly active in pursuing pagans.

The alternative Roma Nova timeline

In AD 395, three months after Theodosius's final decree banning all non-Christian religious activity, four hundred Romans loyal to the old gods, and so in danger of execution, trekked north out of Italy to a semi-mountainous area similar to modern Slovenia. Led by Senator Apulius at the head of twelve prominent families, they established a colony based initially on land owned by Apulius's Celtic father-in-law. By purchase, alliance and conquest, this grew into Roma Nova.

Norman Davies in *Vanished Kingdoms: The History of Half-Forgotten Europe* reminds us that:

> ...in order to survive, newborn states need to possess a set of viable internal organs, including a functioning executive, a defence force, a revenue system and a diplomatic force. If they possess none of these things, they lack the means to sustain an autonomous existence and they perish before they can breathe and flourish.

I would add history, willpower and adaptability as essential factors. Roma Nova survived by changing its social structure; as men constantly fought to defend the new colony, women took over the social, political and economic roles, weaving new power and influence networks based on family structures. Given the unstable, dangerous times in Roma Nova's first few hundred years, daughters as well as sons had to put on armour and heft swords to defend their homeland and their way of life. Fighting for survival side by side with brothers and fathers reinforced women's roles and status.

The Roma Novans never allowed the incursion of monotheistic, paternalistic religions; they'd learnt that lesson from old Rome. Service to the state was valued higher than personal advantage, echoing Roman Republican virtues, and the women heading the families guarded and enhanced these values to provide a core philosophy throughout the centuries. Inheritance passed from these powerful women to their daughters and granddaughters.

Roma Nova's continued existence has been favoured by three factors: the discovery and exploitation of high-grade silver in their mountains, their efficient technology, and their flexible but robust response to any threat. Under pressure from the Eastern Romans, they sent an envoy to stop the Norman invasion of England.

Remembering the Fall of Constantinople, Roma Novan troops assisted at the Battle of Vienna in 1683 to halt the Ottoman advance into Europe. Nearly two hundred years later, they used their diplomatic skills to forge an alliance to push Napoleon IV back across the Rhine as he attempted to expand his grandfather's empire.

Prioritising survival, Roma Nova remained neutral in the Great War of the twentieth century which lasted from 1925 to 1935. The Greater German Empire was broken up afterwards into its former small kingdoms, duchies and counties; some became republics. Today, the tiny country of Roma Nova has become one of the highest per capita income states in the world.

NEXUS gives us a glimpse into Aurelia's life in between two previous stories and also shows why Harry Carter helped her and Roma Nova in *RETALIO*. But that's in the future…

You don't have to have read any of the series to enjoy this story, but I hope that after reading *NEXUS* you'll be tempted to pick up another Roma Nova adventure.

ACKNOWLEDGEMENTS

The indefatigable Denise Barnes (a.k.a. novelist Molly Green), my critique writing partner of ten years, for casting her eagle eyes over the first version I dared to show anybody and giving all my work 'brutal love'.

Helen Hollick and her daughter, Kathy Hollick-Blee of Taw River Show Jumping for making sure I didn't make a horse of myself.

JJ Marsh, crime writer extraordinaire, who very kindly read and endorsed NEXUS and keeps giving me sensible marketing advice.

Jessica Bell Design for her patience and professionalism for designing the cover and fending off my wackier ideas.

Carol Turner, who has copy-edited several Roma Nova stories with firmness but friendliness, and knocked my commas into line.

THE ROMA NOVA THRILLER SERIES

The Carina Mitela adventures

INCEPTIO

Early 21st century. Terrified after a kidnap attempt, New Yorker Karen Brown, has a harsh choice – being terminated by government enforcer Renschman or fleeing to Roma Nova, her dead mother's homeland in Europe. Founded sixteen hundred years ago by Roman exiles and ruled by women, it gives Karen safety, at a price. But Renschman follows and sets a trap she has no option but to enter.

CARINA – A novella

Carina Mitela is still an inexperienced officer in the Praetorian Guard Special Forces of Roma Nova. Disgraced for a disciplinary offence, she is sent out of everybody's way to bring back a traitor from the Republic of Quebec. But when she discovers a conspiracy reaching into the highest levels of Roma Nova, what price is personal danger against fulfilling the mission?

PERFIDITAS

Falsely accused of conspiracy, 21st century Praetorian Carina Mitela flees into the criminal underworld. Hunted by the security services and traitors alike, she struggles to save her beloved Roma Nova as well as her own life. Who is her ally and who her enemy? But the ultimate betrayal is waiting for her…

SUCCESSIO

21st century Praetorian Carina Mitela's attempt to resolve a past family indiscretion is spiralling into a nightmare. Convinced her beloved husband has deserted her, and with her enemy holding a gun to the imperial heir's head, Carina has to make the hardest decision of her life.

The Aurelia Mitela adventures

AURELIA

Late 1960s. Sent to Berlin to investigate silver smuggling, former Praetorian Aurelia Mitela barely escapes a near-lethal trap. Her old enemy is at the heart of all her troubles and she pursues him back home to Roma Nova but he strikes at her most vulnerable point – her young daughter.

INSURRECTIO

Early 1980s. Caius Tellus, the charismatic leader of a rising nationalist movement, threatens to destroy Roma Nova.

Aurelia Mitela, ex-Praetorian and imperial councillor, attempts to counter the growing fear and instability. But it may be too late to save Roma Nova from meltdown and herself from destruction by her lifelong enemy....

RETALIO

Early 1980s Vienna. Aurelia Mitela chafes at her enforced exile. She barely escaped from her nemesis, Caius Tellus, who has grabbed power in Roma Nova.

Aurelia is determined to liberate her homeland. But Caius's manipulations have ensured that she is ostracised by her fellow exiles.

Powerless and vulnerable, Aurelia fears she will never see Roma Nova again.

ROMA NOVA EXTRA

A collection of short stories

Four historical and four present day and a little beyond

A young tribune sent to a backwater in 370 AD for practising the wrong religion, his lonely sixty-fifth descendant labours in the 1980s to reconstruct her country. A Roma Novan imperial councillor attempting to stop the Norman invasion of England in 1066, her 21st century Praetorian descendant flounders as she searches for her own happiness.

Some are love stories, some are lessons learned, some resolve tensions and unrealistic visions, some are plain adventures, but above all, they are stories of people in dilemmas and conflict, and their courage and effort to resolve them.

www.ingramcontent.com/pod-product-compliance
Lightning Source LLC
LaVergne TN
LVHW041708060526
838201LV00043B/625